MW01235916

The Runaway

SHIPWRECK KEY BOOK TWO

STEPHANIE TAYLOR

Prologue

The White House is decorated with giant, glittery pastel eggs and furry stuffed bunnies. A brick walkway that runs along the outside near the back garden is lined with three-tiered topiaries punctuated with daisies and tulips that peek out randomly from between the green leaves like birds perched in trees.

"Ma'am." A woman in a smart suit and sensible shoes nods at Sunday Bond as they pass one another going in opposite directions.

Sunday's heels click against the bricks as she walks at a determined clip, wondering where her husband could be. It's not unusual for Peter Bond, the Vice President of the United States of America, to shuttle himself off to locations unknown and to stay busy for hours doing who knows what. If Sunday were the President—which she's not, obviously —she would call that man on the carpet at every opportunity and demand to know just what he was doing to be worthy of holding such an important job. Because the last time she checked, her work with the homeless shelter in Alexandria has yielded far more coverage and far more results than anything Peter has done during his time in office.

"Julia?" Sunday pauses in a hallway with gorgeous silk butterflies of all sizes and colors hanging from the high ceiling. As people pass

1

beneath them, the butterflies wave and flutter on their invisible strings; spring has truly sprung within the White House.

"Mrs. Bond," Julia says, stopping in her tracks. Julia is short and petite and wears glasses that have bright blue frames—her only concession to fashion, as Julia, like the other female staffers, has had her fashion sense completely neutered by the patriarchy of the political establishment. At least in Sunday's humble opinion.

"Julia, have you seen my husband?" Sunday frowns and tucks a stray curl behind her ear.

At fifty-three, she is still strong and muscled from her five-day-a-week workouts with a yoga and pilates instructor, and her own fashion sense tends to be far more colorful than that of the women who work inside the White House. Today, for instance, Sunday is wearing a belted silk dress in a bright, springy green that shows off her toned figure. She's chosen a pair of patent leather fuchsia high heels with a strap that wraps around the ankle, and on her ears she's wearing pink and green rhinestone drop earrings shaped like flowers.

"Uhhh," Julia says, glancing up and down the hallway, which is empty except for them. "No, I'm sorry, Mrs. Bond. I haven't."

"Okay, thanks." Sunday flashes her a perfunctory smile and walks on, her stride long and purposeful.

In the next wing, Sunday finds a knot of male staffers standing around discussing something in hushed tones. At the sight of the Second Lady they break up, trying unsuccessfully to look as though they're busy with something important.

"Men," Sunday says, stopping short. She puts her hands on her narrow hips and widens her stance, well aware that her bare legs are hard to miss; it's their attention she wants, and even if she has to rely on her looks to get it, she's going to have these men's eyes on her. "Who can point me to where the Vice President is hiding today?"

Five sets of eyes move around the room, studiously avoiding one another as all of the men smile at Sunday graciously.

"Not sure, Mrs. Bond," a young man named Ethan says, straightening his tie. He looks uncomfortable. "I haven't seen him all morning."

Sunday is losing her patience and she knows that at least *one* of these knuckleheads has seen Peter wandering the White House as he munches on a bagel and stands looking up at a painting of a former president like he's some sort of guest or visitor. It's exasperating, tracking Peter down when he doesn't want to be found.

With a sigh, Sunday keeps walking. Now that she's growing truly impatient, her steps are getting louder, her high heels punctuating her walk like the keys on an old-fashioned typewriter hitting the ribbon.

"Peter?" she calls out loudly, peering through open doorways and looking into every alcove. "Peter, it's Easter, for crying out loud. We have hundreds of children with special needs out on the South Lawn, waiting to meet the Easter Bunny, and their parents all want to shake hands with the Vice President, because they were promised a meet and greet." Sunday is saying this all out loud as she walks, stopping every so often and opening a closed door just in case her husband is sitting at a desk, feet propped up as he peruses the sports scores on his phone.

"Peter Langford Bond," Sunday says sharply, her voice raising to the point that she's nearly shouting. "Where the hell are you?"

A woman turns the corner just as Sunday approaches and they nearly collide.

"Oh!" the woman says, a hand flying to her chest as if she's been startled to the verge of a heart attack. "Mrs. Bond. I'm so sorry."

"You heard me coming," Sunday says, sounding as snippy as she feels. "I've been yelling down this damn hallway for the past five minutes." It's completely uncharacteristic for Sunday to lose her cool and snap at a staffer, but her patience is wearing thin as she thinks of all the families outside waiting to meet her and Peter, and she knows that *someone* in this building is covering for him.

"Yes," the woman says, sounding placid and noncommittal. "I understand."

"You do? Then could you please point me toward the last place you saw the Vice President?"

Meekly, the woman turns her body and lifts a hand, pointing in the direction of the kitchen.

"Ha," Sunday says. "I knew food would be involved. It's not like we skipped breakfast, but leave it to Peter to drop by the kitchen and try to sneak a piece of bacon or a muffin." She looks at the woman, whose name escapes her; she's a minor player, and not someone Sunday interacts with often, but Sunday still softens her tone when she realizes that she's taking her anger out on someone who has nothing to do with Peter's behavior. "Thank you. I appreciate your help."

The door to the kitchen swings open as Sunday pushes it with her manicured hand, peeking in slowly as though she might catch Peter shoveling in some snack that's been forbidden by the doctor following his last physical. Things on the list of no-no breakfast items for the Vice President include: full-fat granola; the heavy cream used in hollandaise sauce on his favorite eggs benedict; bacon; sugary pastries and danishes; and pretty much every other delicious thing that Peter loves to shove in his face.

The kitchen is quiet and Sunday sees no one, so she steps all the way inside. The giant slabs of marble that cover the long counters and an enormous island are laden with colorful bowls of fruits and vegetables, and next to the stove is an oversized crate of brown, organic eggs. The clear-doored refrigerator reveals neatly stocked shelves of milk and cream in glass bottles, washed and sorted berries, apples, and lemons, and perfectly stacked containers of yogurt, cream cheese, cottage cheese, butter, and sour cream. There is a pot on the stove, and a large, copper colander in the sink, waiting to strain pasta or rinse veggies or be of some use in the preparation of the food that will end up on tables all throughout the White House.

"Peter?" Sunday tries again, though this time she's not yelling. There's a strange echo to the kitchen that makes Sunday feel like she's not alone. She walks through the long galley where the counters are covered with blenders, two giant mixers with silver bowls, a coffee pot, an espresso machine that looks like a person would need clearance from NASA to run it, and a huge, shiny toaster oven.

"Peter?" Sunday says, but this time it's almost a whisper. Ahead of her is a huge walk-in freezer, and next to that, a pantry door. From beneath the door of the pantry she can see a warm, yellow light.

Sunday stops right outside of the pantry with her hand on the doorknob. She knows this is a make-or-break moment; a turning point in her life that will send her either this way or that. But nothing can stop her now.

She takes a deep breath and opens the door.

There, in the pantry, with their hair and shirts disheveled, hands pushed under fabric and bodies pressed together in a passionate clinch, is Peter, panting heavily in the ear of the White House's head chef.

"Oh my God!" Sunday jumps back and puts a hand over her eyes, though the scene is not graphic enough to warrant true horror. Still, it's a shock to the system to see your husband rubbing his cheek against the neck of another man as they move together in a heated embrace—even if it isn't the first time you've seen it. "Peter, what in the—"

Peter jumps back from Adam, the chef, tugging at his unbuttoned shirt. He looks guilty. Caught. For once, he actually looks scared of Sunday.

"Sunday," Peter says, hastily buttoning his shirt as Adam tugs at the waistband of his own pants, which have been twisted sideways. "You shouldn't have come looking for me."

"I..." she says, shaking her head in disbelief. "I shouldn't have come looking for you? It's Easter, Peter. We're supposed to be on the South Lawn right now, and you're in here with..." She gestures at Adam, unsure of what words will come out of her mouth if she keeps talking.

"Adam," the chef says, looking sheepish and avoiding the Second Lady's gaze.

"Oh, I know your name," Sunday says, putting her fingertips to her temples. Her hands are starting to shake. "Peter," she says, taking a deep, cleansing breath and looking him straight in the eye. "This is the last time I'm going to be humiliated by you. There isn't a man in Washington you haven't locked yourself in a pantry with at this point. When your term is up here in the White House, *our* term is up."

Peter runs his hands through his hair and shakes his head. "What?"

"You heard me: after we leave the White House, I'm divorcing you."

Sunday

The Easter that Sunday found Peter in a compromising position with the chef is now just a fading memory. Since then, they've survived the unexpected death of the President at the very end of his first term, and then their consequential departure from the White House. Normally Peter would have been an immediate shoo-in to the Oval Office following the President's death, but given that his term was just ending when Jack Hudson died, it had left Peter and Sunday to decide whether Peter should run for President himself, or if they should consider a different angle.

In the end, the Vice President's advisors had suggested that he not make his own bid for the White House, given that his popularity rating was much lower than his opponent's, and true to her word, Sunday had filed for divorce.

A quick trip down to Shipwreck Key with Helen Pullman, former Chief of Staff to President Hudson, had convinced Sunday that what she really needed to do was to start over on the tropical island with her close friend, Ruby Hudson—the former First Lady—as her neighbor. So far, Ruby has been on Shipwreck Key for a total of three months, and she's never been happier.

"Mama?" Olive, Sunday's daughter, who was adopted from China as a newborn, is deep in Sunday's closet, digging for a specific dress. "Do you think you left it in storage?"

Sunday is laying on her bed—a giant, fluffy confection of a bed piled high with pillows in every shade of gray imaginable—and she's nibbling on Wheat Thins straight out of the box with her bare feet propped up on a furry pillow.

"I'm not sure, sweets," Sunday says, tipping the cracker box so that she can shove her hand in further. "Do you really need *that* dress, or can we just get you a different one?" The dress in question is a midnight blue shantung sheath dress that hits just above the knee and has spaghetti straps made of rhinestones. Olive has asked to borrow it for a wedding where the bridesmaids have been told to wear any shade of blue they like.

"I remember trying it on when I was a teenager, and I just loved it so much," Olive says, poking her head out of the closet. She's standing there in just a bra and underwear, ready to try on the blue dress when she finds it. "Do you have anything similar that I haven't seen yet?"

Sunday shrugs and eats another salty cracker. "Dunno. I think I gave away a ton of stuff before I came down here. Maybe I got rid of the blue dress after all."

"Mom! No, don't say that! Remember how good you looked in that?"

Does Sunday remember? She looks out her bedroom window at the slice of sky that's visible above the ocean right outside of her house. Of course she remembers wearing that dress. She and Peter had gone to a fundraising event in the Hamptons one summer evening, and she'd shown up wearing that gorgeously cut dress with a pair of earrings that looked like diamond-encrusted stars. Her nails were a glossy red, and on her feet she wore a pair of navy blue Manolo Blahnik strappy heels that made her legs look a thousand miles long. It's one of the only times that Sunday remembers feeling truly beautiful on Peter's arm.

In fact, that night she'd caught him gazing at her across the lawn of the gorgeous old mansion in Sag Harbor as she'd laughed and sipped champagne with a group of women she knew from various charities she'd worked with, and as their eyes locked, Sunday felt for a split second that she'd made the absolute right decision in marrying Peter. Of course that feeling had dissipated by the time they were in the back of their chauffeured car, as Sunday had seen Peter standing by the pool as the sun set, talking closely with one of the many men he'd been rumored to have carried on affairs with over the years, but for a brief moment she'd felt like a wife who was both cherished and admired by her husband.

"I remember sitting on your bed with Cameron while you got ready that night," Olive says now, leaning against the doorframe of the closet and watching her mom wistfully. "You looked like Princess Di."

Sunday sets the half-empty box of Wheat Thins on her nightstand and sits up, brushing her hands together to get the salty crumbs off. "Yeah, I was in Princess Di-level shape at that point of my life," she agrees, reaching for a can of La Croix to wash down the crackers. Cameron, her other daughter, was adopted from Guatemala the same year that Sunday and Peter adopted Olive, though Cameron was already three at the time. The girls are such bright lights in Sunday's life that they alone make her feel as if marrying Peter was the right thing to do. The rightness of their existence in her life is the only thing she's never once questioned—even if Cameron is currently not speaking to her.

"You're still in great shape, Mom," Olive says, turning back to the closet and disappearing again. "You could have any guy you want," she calls out.

Sunday laughs. "I don't know about that, Ollie, and I'm not even sure I want one at this point. They're a lot of work."

"Mom," Olive says, poking her head out again. This time she's holding a black zip-up bag on a hanger in her hands. "Do you think this might be it?"

"Open it. Let's find out." Sunday climbs off her bed and stretches her arms overhead.

"Oh," Olive says, sounding reverent as she unzips the bag. Inside is the fabled blue dress. "It's still as beautiful as I remember."

"Yes," Sunday says, reaching out and unzipping the bag the rest of the way. She pulls out the dress and takes it off the hanger, holding it out for her daughter. "Believe it or not, a dress worn once and stored properly can hold up quite nicely. Here you go, babe." She hands it to Olive. "Let's see you in it."

When Olive emerges again with the dress on, she makes a beeline for the full-length mirror. Sunday steps up behind her and zips the dress carefully, watching her daughter's face in the mirror from over Olive's shoulder.

"You look gorgeous, Ollie. I love it."

Olive is rapt; she's admiring her own image and the way the dress hugs her thin body, pushing her breasts up and elongating her ribcage. "Is it really okay if I borrow it?" she asks in a whisper.

"Darling, you can keep it. I don't mind if I never see that dress again, because honestly, after seeing how stunning you are in it, am I ever going to be able to zip my old lady bod into it again?" She swats Olive's firm bottom and walks away to find the star-shaped diamond earrings in her jewelry box to loan her daughter.

"Thank you, Mom. It's perfect," Olive says, sounding pleased. "And you would still look amazing in this dress, so knock it off."

Sunday chuckles. Sure, she might still be able to pull off wearing the dress, but to what end? And what for? Life on Shipwreck Key has proven to be a blissfully casual affair: gray t-shirts, running shorts, flip-flops, and maybe the occasional sundress have been Sunday's wardrobe staples. She's completely stopped wearing foundation, she doesn't bother to blow dry or flat-iron her hair, and she never wears anything that doesn't make her feel comfortable.

"Thanks, babe," Sunday says to Olive as she hands her the earrings. "These I want back, but the dress is yours. If I ever need something formal again, I'll just buy something new."

Sunday picks up the box of Wheat Thins and her empty La Croix can and heads downstairs, leaving her daughter in front of the mirror, turning this way and that. Unlike Ruby's gigantic, five-bedroom house on the water, Sunday has chosen something far more sedate. It's a cute two-story, three-bedroom house on the beach, and the thing Sunday loves about it the most—other than its coziness—is the long wooden boardwalk that leads across the sand and up to her front porch. She'd never imagined having a place of her own with a view of the ocean, and the sense of freedom that the house gives her is beyond measure.

The sink in her kitchen looks directly onto the beach, and Sunday stands there now, rinsing the few dishes that she's left there from break-fast. Even this small task is something she won't take for granted, because there have been years and years of living in posh townhouses with housekeepers on hand to pick up after her, and many more years where her days were filled with getting ready for events, delegating tasks, and making sure that her daughters were being picked up and ferried to dance lessons, piano recitals, and soccer matches. This chance to bumble around her own house, doing what she wants to do at her leisure is a novelty that hasn't yet worn off for Sunday.

She shakes the water off a coffee mug that she's just rinsed and sets it in the top rack of her dishwasher, keeping an eye on the way the ocean moves rhythmically before her. It's hypnotic, really, and she can foresee spending hours and hours at the sink, washing and re-washing things as she daydreams and looks at the waves.

Peter never loved the beach like she does. If some people are beach people, and some people are mountains people, then Peter would be best categorized as a city person. Getting him to vacation for the girls' sake wasn't impossible, and over the years they'd been to nearly every Disney park on the planet, to London and Paris when the girls were teenagers, and to tropical resorts that boasted privacy and relaxation, but in truth never truly brought either. Life with Peter was always about optics, strategy, and politics, and while Sunday had (fairly) willingly signed on for all that, there had been many, many moments that she'd regretted doing so. But what had her options been? She can chastise herself all she wants now, but she knows that while her life as Second Lady came with some steep costs, it also saved her from a totally different fate.

She picks up a towel and wipes her wet counter, then leans over the sink to look at the flowers she has sitting in neat little pots on her windowsill. Even having the time and patience to nurture tiny sprigs of nasturtiums and African violets is a wonder to Sunday, and she smiles as she touches the damp soil. She's about to start her dishwasher and run a load when a figure out on the beach catches her eye: it's Banks, Ruby's Secret Service agent, jogging along the hard-packed sand next to the water. Unlike the former First Lady, a former Second Lady isn't assured Secret Service protection after her husband's time in office is up, but Sunday certainly enjoys the sight of this particular member of Ruby's security detail, and she always has.

Sunday drops the dishtowel onto the counter and leans her hips against the sink, craning her neck to watch Banks's firm, toned body as he jogs—shirtless, mind you—along the deserted beach. She stands up straight once Banks is out of her view and glances around to make sure that Olive hasn't tiptoed into the kitchen and caught her mother ogling a half-dressed man, but she's still alone, so Sunday goes back to poking her flower pots and wiping her already clean counters.

People have always been curious about Sunday's romantic life, and for damn good reason. It's an open secret in Washington that Peter Bond is gay, and throughout the course of their marriage he'd made almost no concessions to the fact that he had a wife and two young daughters at home, dating openly among the pool of handsome, young, social-climbing gay men in the city—and around the world, for that matter. Sunday had first caught him in bed with another man in their own home, and the sheer shock that had rocked her world at that moment was something she'd never truly experienced again. Once you've seen your husband canoodling with another man for the first time, even the worst horror movie imaginable kind of pales in comparison.

After catching Peter and young William, a clean-cut Congressional aide who was half Peter's age, she'd regularly stumbled into rooms and caught Peter having phone or text conversations with other men, and the jokes that people made when they thought she wasn't listening were enough to humiliate even the toughest broad. But Sunday wasn't tough —at least not then—though she is now. She's learned over the years to distance herself from Peter, from his actions, and from anything that doesn't directly pertain to her own survival and that of her daughters.

And her daughters...what joy they've brought to Sunday's life! She wanders over to the glass-fronted cabinets in her kitchen, running her fingers over the bubbled surface that reminds her of sea glass. She stares at the cups and glasses in varying shades of blue and green as she thinks of Olive and Cameron. Olive, with her long, almost waist-length dark hair and knowing eyes. She's defied the odds over the years, coming to Sunday and Peter as a newborn with a small hole in her heart that required surgery and many sleepless nights. Sunday is afraid that she babied Olive too much over the years, never forcing her to really push herself, but now that she's twenty-seven, Olive is a lovely, gentle soul with her own cute little bakery in the small Connecticut town where she's living with her boyfriend, James.

It's Cameron who gives Sunday heartburn. At thirty, Cameron is angry. She doesn't understand why Sunday put up with Peter's shenanigans for as many years as she did, and as a strong feminist, she thinks that her mother's actions are directly responsible for sending a negative message to other women. They'd argued about it the Thanksgiving before Sunday caught Peter and Adam together in the pantry of the White House kitchen, but even Sunday finally serving Peter with divorce papers hadn't thawed Cameron's heart toward her mother.

"Cammy," Sunday whispers to herself now, looking out at the September sky. She'd always loved Cameron's strong sense of womanhood, but sometimes she wished that her daughter would set it aside for one minute and understand that life is full of gray areas; not everything is black or white.

"Hey, Mom?" Olive calls out as she descends the wooden staircase, which creaks slightly beneath her bare feet. "Are you hungry?"

A smile spreads across Sunday's face. She's just eaten her weight in Wheat Thins, but she no longer cares how many carbs she's snacking on, or whether she's gotten up on time to meet her trainer for five-thirty weight training sessions every weekday morning followed by an hour of yoga.

"I could eat," Sunday says, turning her back to the kitchen window and looking at Olive, who has switched out the midnight blue dress for a pair of white shorts and a yellow t-shirt. "You want me to make something?"

Olive laughs out loud. "Mom. I love you, but you don't cook. In fact, I have no idea how you're going to survive down here without having every restaurant you're used to ordering from within a few miles from your house."

Sunday sticks out her tongue and makes a face. "The Frog's Grog does takeout. And so does The Black Pearl."

"Oooh, let's go there," Olive says, pulling her long hair back and fastening it with a claw clip. "Can we wear shorts and flip-flops?"

Sunday glances down at her own casual attire. "On Shipwreck Key," she says, "you can wear anything you want."

* * *

The Black Pearl is situated at the end of Seadog Lane, Shipwreck Key's main street. There's a sandy lot carved out in front of the restaurant, and it's filled with golf carts parked haphazardly in unmarked spots. The restaurant itself juts out over the water, its wooden deck high enough that it makes outdoor diners feel like they're floating on the edge of a cruise ship as they dine on lobster rolls, grouper and chips, cracked conch, and island curried shrimp.

Sunday walks up to the hostess stand with her Birkenstocks slapping against the wooden slats of the deck. She hasn't bothered to change out of her shorts and t-shirt, and instead of combing her hair and putting on mascara, she's hidden her hair under a hat and shielded her makeup-free eyes behind sunglasses.

"Table for two, Mrs. Bond?" the young girl with the menus smiles at her. Under different circumstances it might annoy Sunday to be recognized while out of the house looking like she just woke up, but in her new life, she couldn't possibly care less.

"Yes, just us two," Sunday says with a huge smile. She hangs onto the strap of her purse over one shoulder as she follows the girl to their table right at the edge of the deck. A nice breeze is blowing in off the water, ruffling Olive's fine, black hair as she pulls out a chair and sits down. "Thank you," Sunday says, taking her menu and flipping it open.

"I think I'm going to go with the Key lime mahi-mahi," Olive says, closing her menu. "And a glass of rosé."

"Sounds delicious." Sunday sets her menu on the edge of the table. "I'll do the same."

Olive digs through her purse for a pair of sunglasses and then puts them on. It's late in the afternoon—not quite dinnertime—but they slept in, skipped lunch, and there's no question that the two women will stay up late watching movies and snacking on popcorn and chocolate on Sunday's couch together, so eating lunch or dinner or whatever meal this is at a random time means nothing to them.

The waitress comes by, takes their order, and whisks their menus away.

"Mom?"

Sunday is resting her chin in her hands as she watches a boat moving across the water out toward the horizon. "Mmhmm?"

"Are you okay?" Olive asks, sounding far younger than she is.

Sunday's turns her head so that she's looking at her youngest daughter instead of at the water. "Honey, yes. Of course. Why? Do I not seem okay?"

Olive shrugs her narrow shoulders. "You just packed up and moved down here so fast, and now that you're here, you seem like...well, you don't seem like Sunday Bond anymore."

This makes Sunday laugh. "Oh?" She watches Olive's face. "Who do I seem like?"

"I mean, you, obviously, but you're just so laid-back here. I've never once in my life seen you go out in a pair of Birkenstocks and a baseball cap." Olive frowns as she looks at her mom's hat, made of a sun-bleached blue denim material with "Oregon Coast" embroidered across the front.

"Well, babe," Sunday says, leaning her elbows on the table and then pausing as the waitress drops off two glasses of rosé. "The new me is really the old me, you just never met the old me before."

"Okayyyy." Olive sips her wine, looking mildly concerned about her mother's well-being.

"No, really," Sunday assures her as they clink their wine glasses together. "I married your father when I was twenty-two, but before that, I was Sunday Bellows. I grew up on one of the least glamorous islands you'll ever see—"

"I know, I know," Olive says, holding her wine glass by its stem. "Tangier Island. So close, and yet so far."

"You have no idea, babe," Sunday says, leveling a serious gaze at her daughter. "It might sound quaint to you, hearing about some tiny island off the coast of Virginia where people still speak with a British accent like we're living in Colonial times, but it's desolate. Your grandfather was a tough, weathered, old fisherman with a mean streak, and your grandmother was just trying to survive and raise her children. When my brother died, my mom disappeared into herself entirely. Your aunt Minnie and I were left to our own devices." Sunday shivers, remembering how cold her house and her life had felt after Jensen drowned when his fishing boat capsized in the freezing Atlantic. To this day, when she's asked about her siblings, she still says she has "a brother and a sister," though it's been about forty years since she last laid eyes on her brother.

"Okay, but Cammy and I were left to our own devices a lot, too," Olive counters, leaning back as the waitress sets their main dishes on the table. "Thank you," she says, smiling at the waitress before turning back to her mom. "You and dad were *really* busy when we were kids. We had nannies for most of our childhoods."

Sunday picks up her knife and fork and shakes her head. "Ollie, being looked after by nannies in a gorgeous home in Washington D.C. while attending private school is *nothing* like looking after yourself in a remote fishing village where your family has no money and most kids don't have a particularly bright future. I wanted to get out of there as fast as I could—and I did. For a lot of different reasons."

Olive chews her first bite of mahi-mahi as she looks out at the water just over the railing. Once she's swallowed and washed it down with a sip of rosé, she looks back at Sunday. "So then you ran away from Tangier Island to live a big life in Washington D.C., only to run away from your big life there to live on a tiny island again?"

Sunday takes a big, long swig of her wine and then rubs her lips together as she savors the taste. "Hell yes, baby." She sets her glass on the table with a clink. "I went from a small island to a big city and then back to a small island again. And that right there is what we call 'coming full circle.'"

Ruby
~∽∽∽

After six months on Shipwreck Key, Ruby Hudson has found her groove. Marooned With a Book, the little shop she's opened on Seadog Lane, brings her the kind of happiness she could have only dreamed of during her years as the faithful First Lady to the late President Jack Hudson. She's got her gorgeous, *Architectural Digest*-worthy house on the beach, her two wonderful daughters living there with her, and the bookstore she wakes up every morning excited to walk into.

Given the fact that her husband had died unexpectedly at the end of his first term in office, that he'd had a mistress and a twelve-year-old son tucked away in France, and that Ruby had been forced to wait a full year after his death to find out that he'd actually taken his own life in order to avoid a painful and rapid deterioration to his health due to a rare neurological disease, she's really doing quite well. Adding to the stress of all that is the horrifying bar shooting that her youngest daughter was caught up in, and the heartbreak her older daughter had gone through at the hands of a man she'd really liked. When you consider everything, Ruby's had quite a year so far. And this is only September.

"We need more books on serial killers," Tilly Byer says, walking through Marooned With a Book wearing a pair of red tartan plaid pants festooned with silver chains that dangle from one belt loop to the next.

Her black hair is twisted into little knots all over her head, and she's wearing red lipstick speckled with shiny glitter. Tilly, the granddaughter of the owner of the bar across the street from the bookshop, is a dyed-in-the-wool goth. She's tough, unflinching, cool, and fully committed to the lifestyle, though Ruby knows enough about teenage girls to know that at least some of Tilly's swagger is just bark with no bite to back it up.

Ruby frowns. "We don't get a lot of requests for true crime novels or books on serial killers," she counters, pulling hardcover copies of the latest Emily Giffin novel from a box on the front counter. She needs to scan them all into the system and set up a display, and Tilly is her side-kick for the day. "But if there's something in particular you want to order and then use your employee discount to buy, you know I'm okay with that, Til."

"I'm thinking of going by 'Matilda' now," Tilly says, segueing into this new topic without preamble. "Tilly sounds too much like a girl who would listen to Coldplay and cry over some boy who won't text her back."

Ruby lifts an eyebrow and adds five more hardcovers to her growing stack. She knows that anything new by an extremely popular author will fly off the shelves. "Oh? Is Coldplay out?"

Tilly snorts. "They're elevator music now. The kind of stuff you hear at the grocery store. Hard pass."

"Mmm," Ruby says, focusing on the task at hand.

"So, is Dexter North coming to the island again soon?" Tilly leans her elbows on the front counter and her studded bracelets clink against the wood. "He's cute. You two should hook up."

Ruby has spent enough time with her own daughters, who are twenty-two and twenty-three, to know that by "hook up" Tilly doesn't just mean "meet up for a drink." This time both of her eyebrows go up.

"I mean, come on," Tilly says, standing up again and resting just her fingertips on the counter. "He's hot. You're single and you've still got it. You two could be a total power couple."

This makes Ruby laugh and she knocks a jar of pencils off the counter and onto the floor. "Oh, Tilly," she says, shaking her head as she bends over to pick up the pencils. "I'm not sure if I'm ready to start thinking about all that stuff."

"So you're not into men?"

Ruby laughs again, nearly dropping the pencils she's just gathered. "I am. But let's talk about you—do you have a boyfriend?"

Tilly makes a disgusted face. "God, no. I prefer women."

Ruby nods and sets the pencils in the cup. "Do you have a girl-friend, then?"

"No, there's no one datable on this island." Tilly rests her elbows on the counter again and gazes out the window at Seadog Lane. "I've known everyone here for most of my life, so dating any of them would feel like I was dating my own cousin." Her upper lip curls as she considers this. "Ruby, what would you do if one of your daughters was into girls?"

Ruby walks a stack of biographies over to a display table. "I would love them just like I love them now," she says, glancing back over her shoulder at Tilly. "It would make no difference to me, as long as they were happy."

Tilly chews on her glittery lower lip and uses her tongue to move the little stud that's pierced right below her lip line as she thinks. "My grandpa thought it was weird the first time I told him I liked girls."

This is delicate territory, and Ruby doesn't want to overstep her bounds. "I'm sorry to hear that," she says, sliding a stack of books aside so that she can set up the new ones. "Has he gotten used to the idea?"

Tilly shrugs. "He's kind of old-school about things. I think he hopes that I'll outgrow it, but honestly, no matter what he says, I know he loves me. He's just a salty old pirate, and he doesn't like it when things change."

"I've gathered that much about him," Ruby says, sinking down onto the floor and sitting criss-cross as she sorts through yet another box of books. For a relatively small island, the residents of Shipwreck Key are avid readers, and Ruby does a brisk business and works hard to keep everything in stock that she knows people will want to read. "But your grandpa is a good man, and he clearly loves this island and he loves you. So I think you should just keep being who you are, and know that he'll catch up with you in his own time. Trust me."

Tilly walks behind the counter and starts to scan in the Emily Giffin books so that they don't have to make eye contact, but Ruby can see the hint of a pleased smile on her face. "So, back to Dexter—when is he coming to the island again?"

Ruby chuckles at this; she has been spending a fair amount of time with the man who is writing a book about her husband and his presidency through the eyes of the First Lady. "Actually, he's been here, we've met on Christmas Key, and now he's asked me to meet him in New York City in a few weeks so we can have another sit-down interview."

"Ooooh, a date in the big city. Nice," Tilly says, tapping at the computer keys.

"Well, not really a date, Til. More like a business meeting."

Tilly rolls her eyes, trying to look bored. "Uh huh."

"No, seriously. Dexter North is a biographer with a job to do, and I'm merely a part of his story." She shrugs helplessly from her spot on the floor, feeling her cheeks go pink as she imagines Dexter's handsome face. "Nothing more, nothing less."

"He's into you. Come on. Add two and two together and come up with four already, Ruby." Tilly slaps a hardcover on the counter after scanning it.

Her lack of concern while talking to a woman who most people speak to with deference and reverence is absolutely refreshing to Ruby. Far from being offended when Tilly just says it like it is, or speaks to Ruby like they've known each other for years, she's absolutely charmed and it secretly thrills her.

"He's thirty-six, honey, and I'm almost fifty. That's not exactly a natural fit."

"It is if you say it is." Tilly stacks another book after scanning it.

Ruby wants to argue this and point out to Tilly that life sometimes doesn't work as smoothly as you'd like it to, but instead she just nods. Who's to say that a nineteen-year-old girl *doesn't* have some wisdom to impart? If there's one thing that Ruby learned by traveling the world and meeting all kinds of people, it's that everyone has something to teach you. *Everyone*. Sometimes you just need to shut up and listen.

"You're right," she says to Tilly. "I'm imposing limits on myself and it's totally unnecessary. I guess we all do that sometimes, don't we?" She looks at her young employee meaningfully.

"Let me guess," Tilly says dryly. "This is some sort of teachable moment. You want me to understand that I'm imposing limits on myself by dressing in a way that's off-putting to everyone on the island, including anyone who might be datable for me, right?"

Caught, Ruby shrugs guiltily. "Well. Maybe. I would imagine in a much bigger city that your look might go over more easily. But here...it just seems like you intentionally want to hold people at bay. And if I'm wrong, tell me I'm wrong."

Tilly purses her lips and narrows her eyes. "I'm not going to say that you're wrong," she says after a beat. "But I am going to think about that before I give a response. Because maybe we all do things to keep other people out, right? Maybe you moved down here to an island full of crusty fishermen, widows, and retired rich couples because you thought you could get lost in the crowd. Then you never have to worry about being asked out by another politician, or going through the kind of crap your husband put you through ever again."

"You're very astute," Ruby says, pushing herself up onto her knees and then standing. "I'll give you that, young lady." She smiles at Tilly and then motions to her little upstairs office, where she retreats sometimes midday to answer emails from Ursula, her virtual assistant, or to just decompress and catch up on what's happening in the world by scrolling through her favorite news outlets. "Could you keep scanning those new books into the system while I handle a few emails?"

"You got it, boss," Tilly says, giving her a sloppy salute.

Upstairs, Ruby switches on the lamp that sits on the corner of her desk and sits at her computer. The room is like a tiny attic hideaway with a sloped ceiling, and her desk sits facing a window made of blue and white stained glass in a fleur-de-lis pattern. She types in the password and brings up her email. The last one from Dexter is the one where he proposed a trip to New York in October so that they could cover a few things over the course of three long days, rather than chopped up into Zoom calls late in the evenings, as they normally do.

So far, she hasn't replied to his invitation, though the minute she read it she started having visions of herself in a chunky sweater and

21

boots, drinking a coffee by the window of a chic cafe as crisp leaves blow by under a blue sky. Autumn in New York is magical, and the invitation had tempted her immediately, but the deeper implications of it had held her back from responding.

She re-reads the email now, parsing it for meaning:

Ruby--

I hope this isn't too much of an ask, but I'd love it if we could do a long weekend in NYC. Hear me out: you could stay anywhere that suits you and I would come to you. We can enjoy the city and the restaurants as we go over some of the topics we've set aside for a time when we have longer to talk. No pressure, and I'd work around your schedule, but I'm thinking early October. I have a draft of the first four chapters I'd love to share with you as well--but in person, so we can talk about them and consider any changes together. Thoughts?

--Dexter

Surely there isn't any deeper meaning--he's just asking her to come up to New York and sit down with him so they can cover the timeline of Jack's death, more of what she knows of his relationship with Etienne, and probably how she really felt the first time she met Jack and Etienne's son, Julien. None of these are wounds that she's dying to pour salt into, but she knows that it will be necessary to address these topics at some point, and possibly the sooner the better.

With a sigh, Ruby pulls out her Day Planner (she still prefers writing things down by hand, no matter how many times her daughters or her assistant beg her to put everything into her phone calendar), and flips through the next few weeks. She picks up a pen and taps the end of it on the first week of October. It's wide open at the moment.

Ruby sets the pen down and puts her fingers on the keyboard.

Dexter--

Apologies for my delay in responding, but I needed to check my schedule. Would the first week of October work for you? I would fly into the city and stay at the Conrad Downtown. I can get a suite that would provide us with a sitting area to talk if necessary, but I think I'd really love to combine the heaviness of our discussions with some more fun activities. It's going to be hard to talk about some of this, but I think I'm ready. It's time.

--Ruby

She hits send and then puts her pen inside the Day Planner between the pages for the first and second week of October, closing the black leather book and setting it on the desk blotter. Every day feels like an exercise in picking up the pieces and moving forward; every day is another opportunity to grow into the new version of Ruby Hudson that she wants to be.

In fact, she's begun to think of herself as Ruby Dallarosa again more often--this is her maiden name, and one she hasn't used in nearly twenty-five years--and she finds that, at least in her mind, it suits her. She may never be able to leave Ruby Hudson behind completely, nor does she want to, but Ruby can begin to move more in the direction of her old self so that she can find the sweet spot between who she is, who she was, and who she wants to be.

Sunday

"So, we just finished reading *Park Avenue Summer*," Ruby says to the book club, holding her own hardcover copy in her hands. Little flags and post-it notes stick out from every angle. "I have to say, I loved this look back at Manhattan in the mid-sixties, and I thought the whole culture of working at a women's magazine was fascinating."

Joining Ruby's book club had been a no-brainer for Sunday: she loves to read, she loves to chat with other women, and so far, she deeply loves Shipwreck Key and wants to be a part of everything that goes on there.

Marigold Pim, former supermodel, current spokeswoman of all things pertaining to aging gracefully and without judgment, stands up and walks over to the table at the side of the room where they always set up their snacks and drinks on book club night.

"Helen Gurley Brown had balls the size of cantaloupes," Marigold says, picking up a napkin and filling it with herb and cheese baked crackers. "She brought the sexual revolution into women's homes by writing boldly about sex and empowerment. I know this book is technically historical fiction, but I felt inspired reading about a real-life figure who did so much for the women's movement. It made me want to go out and conquer a man--any man--and plant my flag on him." She pops a cracker into her mouth and crunches it happily.

"Some of it was pretty over-the-top for me," Molly, the owner of The Scuttlebutt, Shipwreck Key's coffee shop/unofficial water cooler, says with a dubious look in Marigold's direction. Molly is in her sixties, wears no makeup, and believes in living her life without frills or artifice. She's been a widow for forty years, her heart is as big as the wide open sea, and she's quickly become an integral part of the book club. "I mean, did women really need to start wearing skirts so short that they flashed their business at everyone?"

Athena, Ruby's older daughter, clears her throat. "I would argue that women should have *always* been able to wear whatever they wanted to wear. This idea that we're opening ourselves up to sexual advances from men when we're not dressing to please them in the first place just feeds into toxic rape culture."

Molly rears back in shock. "Now, I know I've been living on a rock in the sea for my whole life here, but 'toxic rape culture'? Honey, this is a fact as old as time and it will never change, whether you young women like it or not: you have to dress the way you want to be treated. It's the same as dressing for success in the workplace—you do that because you want to be taken seriously in a man's world, right? Well, I say the same thing applies in every aspect of your life: if you dress like you've got something for sale, you're going to be treated that way."

Tilly's eyebrows are nearly in her hairline, and Vanessa, who is Ruby's more sweet and innocent bookstore employee, looks like a fish gasping for air on dry land.

"Are you saying that we all dress like hoes?" Harlow, Ruby's younger daughter, asks. Her nostrils are slightly flared.

"No," Molly says firmly, shaking her head. "I'm saying that you can't change human nature. If you put your goods in front of a man, he's going to see you a certain way even if you've been bestowed with the biggest brain on the planet. Men are simple that way, honey--if you show them boobs, they think 'boobs.' I hate to be the bearer of bad news, but facts are facts."

After nibbling quietly on a plate of crackers and spinach dip while she nurses a glass of Chardonnay, Sunday finally speaks up.

"Ladies," she says, looking as laid-back as if someone has just roused her from a relaxing bubble bath, "you can do everything right—you can dress the way they want you to, say the right things, and act like a perfect lady—but you're still going to have people wiping their feet on your back. So while I'm old enough to agree whole-heartedly with Molly, I'm also of the mind that our younger women are getting it right by giving the middle finger to the patriarchy." She shrugs and takes another sip of her wine. "I just don't think I care anymore what anybody believes about me." Ruby is shooting her a pointed look, but Sunday doesn't even register the arched eyebrow. "I'm the perfect example: I did it all the way everyone wanted and expected me to, and I still spent three decades married to a man who couldn't keep it zipped."

Athena chokes on the sip of Diet Coke that she's just taken and Harlow leans over and whacks her on the back unceremoniously.

"But Aunt Sun," Athena says again when she's cleared her airway. "Nothing your husband did had anything to do with how *you* acted. You have to know that, right?"

Sunday waves a hand through the air lazily and stands up, wandering to the front window with her wine glass in hand. For this evening, she's dressed in a pair of black leggings, a black bodysuit, and a long, flowing chiffon vest in a swirl of pinks and blues that reaches her calves and floats on the air as she walks. She's wearing black platform sandals with an ankle strap, and a huge pair of pink amethyst stud earrings. So far, Ruby's book club meetings have been the only thing that gets Sunday to take off her running shorts and flip-flops, and she actually enjoys digging through her closet to find something fun to wear to these evenings of wine and book talk.

"All I know," Sunday says, standing with her back to the group as she watches a middle-aged couple walking two Golden Retrievers on red leashes outside on Seadog Lane, "is that I went into marriage and moth-erhood thinking that I'd be spending my fifties like those people right there." She nods at the couple as they look both ways for speeding golf carts and then cross the street to sit outside at a bistro table at The Frog's Grog. "I didn't think I'd be humiliated over and over and over again by the man I'd sworn to be faithful to."

When Sunday turns around, the other women are staring at her, and Ruby is looking at her with real concern.

"I feel like I could say, without hesitation, that every one of us sitting here in this room has hit a speed bump or two, Sun," Ruby says. "Not a one of us has traveled a completely smooth path, and we've all had things happen that, arguably, *shouldn't* have happened to us."

Sunday looks out the window again, feeling strangely detached. She's still holding her wine glass in one hand, and with the other, she lifts the chiffon of her long vest and swirls it around her body absent-mindedly. She wishes that Olive could have stayed longer on Shipwreck Key; she came down for a long weekend, found the dress she wanted, and then headed back to Connecticut and her life there with James and the bakery. Olive always seems to think her bakery will fall apart without her there to roll the dough and fill the pastries, which is charming but probably untrue. Still, Sunday admires her dedication.

And Cameron...where is Cameron right now? If Sunday could ask her, would Cammy say that she felt as if life had steamrolled her at some point? That the universe had failed to recognize the fact that she was doing everything right? She would love to know, to sit down with Cameron and talk, really talk, like two grown women, and not like a mother and a disappointed daughter.

"This is the hard part, Sun," Ruby says, walking across the store as the other ladies sip their drinks and stay quiet. Ruby stands behind Sunday and puts her hands on her shoulders. "You filed for divorce in the spring and moved down here three months ago," she says gently. "It's totally normal that the initial excitement of the move and of buying a house would have worn off a little. Now is when the doubts creep in and nag at you: *Did I do the right thing? Are my daughters proud of me? Do I even know what I'm doing?*" Ruby pauses for a minute, her hands still on Sunday's shoulders as she stands behind her. "I just want you to know that I think you're incredibly brave, and that you're not going through this big life change alone. You have me no matter what."

Sunday turns to look at Ruby gratefully, tears filling her eyes. "Thanks, Rubes," she whispers, pulling her friend into a tight hug.

Molly lifts her wine glass. "You've got the rest of us, too. Might be a helluva lot more than you bargained for when you moved down here, but if you want a rusty old anchor like me, a woman who's never taken a bad photo," she glances at Marigold, "a lady who'll marry your dad if he's still alive," she lifts her glass at Heather Charleton-Bicks, who guffaws at this unexpected barb, "and a bunch of young lassies who are out to change the world," she nods at Vanessa, Tilly, Harlow, and Athena, "then you've got yourself a proper girl gang here on Shipwreck Key."

The young women fall into fits of laughter at this, even Tilly, who isn't prone to cracking a smile if it isn't in response to a sarcastic joke. Harlow stands up, ready to propose a toast.

"Aunt Sunday," Harlow says, smoothing down the front of her satiny yellow shorts, which she's paired with a tiny, cropped denim jacket and worn-in cowboy boots. Her hair is untamed, and she's wearing a slash of shiny fuchsia lipstick. "You've come to the right place. Trust me. When I showed up here after that whole..." she waves one hand around, looking uncomfortable, "bar shooting incident, I didn't know how I was going to pull myself together again. I saw people *die*, and it was horrible." She pauses to collect herself. "But this bookstore and these women have been like my backbone." Sunday is looking right at Harlow as she talks, and Harlow goes on. "We can all be that for you, if you need us to."

Sunday's tears have spilled over, and she nods, crying openly. "Yeah," she says, smiling through her tears. "I do need that. I really think I do."

* * *

The reason for Sunday's uncharacteristic pensiveness is sitting on her kitchen table at home. When she gets back from book club, she drops her purse and keys on the little white wood table by the front door, turning on the lamp next to the dish where she leaves her keys, which is made of half of a giant clamshell. Her front room, small and cozy as it is, is warmed by the lamplight. The small gray loveseat is set against the wall to make the most of the view out onto the sand, and over the back of the couch is a hand-knitted chenille blanket, made by Sunday's sister Minnie when the girls were still toddlers.

Sunday takes off her long, chiffon vest, and replaces it by wrapping the chenille blanket from the couch around her shoulders. She kicks off her shoes and heads over to the dining table, which is tucked into a corner of her kitchen. She likes to think of it as her breakfast nook, and she tries not to compare it to the massive kitchen that Ruby has, with its huge picture windows looking straight at the ocean—as she sits at her small, round table.

The laptop hums to life when Sunday opens it, and since the only light she's turned on is the lamp on the table in the entryway, her face is lit almost entirely by the glow of her computer screen as she navigates to her email. She's already read the message three times, but she skims it again.

I feel like I'm the bearer of bad news lately...first having to rush down to Shipwreck Key to tell Ruby about the book, and now having to tell you this, though I think you'll be glad it's coming from me. Peter has been shopping a story around to various outlets about how you're frigid, and that the end of your marriage is your fault, and yours alone. Sorry to be so brutal, hon, but I want you to hear it like it is, and it ain't good. I know you're down there now, living a whole different life that's mercifully removed from Washington and from the public eye, but you have daughters—you have family. I wouldn't want you to be blindsided by him sharing your personal secrets with the world, and Sunday, I think he's going to share them all. Starting with everything that happened on Tangier Island. I'm so sorry—please tell me if there's anything at all that I can do.

Yours, always—

Helen

Poor Helen. She'd been Jack Hudson's Chief of Staff, and from there, had become a dear and beloved friend of both Ruby and Sunday's. An alliance as strong as theirs formed between women in Washington is unusual—perhaps it's unusual in any place that trades on power as currency—but time and time again, Helen has shown the former First and Second Ladies that she has their backs. That her friendship is not conditional on whether they're still a part of the political machine that is Washington D.C. Any one of the three women would move mountains for the other two, and Sunday knows that it will always be this way between them.

But now, Helen having to be the one to let Sunday know that her deepest, darkest secrets might come out as part of her divorce proceedings makes her cringe. And for what—so that Peter can spin the narrative in his favor? So that he can restore the golden glow to his own reputation and potentially use that in future bids for an office of some sort? At sixty, Peter Bond is still handsome and charming in the way that politicians can be, but in Sunday's eyes, he's nothing but a man who hides behind a mask. In public, he pretends to be a smooth, moneyed gentleman with a gorgeous family, but when the mask drops, he's the kind of husband who belittles his wife, leaves her in hotel rooms as he combs dark bars for quick, meaningless interludes with other men, and who would now trot out the skeletons in his wife's closet and jeeringly dance with them in front of the world because it makes him look good. It makes her sick to think that she's spent thirty years of her life married to a man like Peter.

With the warm chenille throw still wrapped around her like a shawl, Sunday walks through her kitchen barefoot and takes a stemless wine goblet from her cupboard. She uncorks the bottle of half-drunk merlot sitting next to her clean sink and pours three swallows into her glass, which she downs like a hearty shot of whiskey before pouring another.

There's a door in her kitchen that leads out to a small back deck, and Sunday lets herself out with her wine glass in hand. She wanders down onto the sand, holding onto the blanket around her shoulders as she thinks about Helen's email. She wouldn't put it past Peter to do exactly what he's threatening to do: throw the mother of his children under the bus in order to elevate his standing in the public eye. It's almost funny to her now to think about what must have gone through her head when she married Peter Bond. Was she so desperate for stability and for a life far beyond the one she would have had on Tangier Island? Yes, of course she was—the answer has to be yes.

Sunday had grown up rough and without even the faintest whisper of glamour or prosperity. The things she'd gone through following her brother's death had been life-altering, and the very thought of those things being used by her soon-to-be ex-husband as a means to an end disgusts her. In some ways, it feels like even more a betrayal of their marriage vows than finding out that Peter had been intimate with other men. After all, if bodies aren't sacred in a marriage--and in so many cases they're not--then at the very least, aren't a person's secrets meant to be safe?

Sunday walks all the way to the edge of the water, looking out at the navy blue sea with its whitecaps. Far off in the distance she can see the lights of a giant cruise ship, and she wonders where it's headed; do the people aboard have secrets buried as deeply as Sunday has buried hers? For all the years Sunday has spent being upbeat, bubbly, and in search of the bright side of any dark cloud, she's also spent an equal amount of time trying to run from the things she can't live with every day.

In spite of the warmth of the September evening, Sunday shivers under the chenille cape she's made for herself. She puts her wine glass to her lips and sips it, blinking back tears under the moonlight. *This is just a temporary setback*, she tells herself. For three decades, she's been able to shake herself off after every fall, hold her shoulders and head high, and push forward with a smile, and she'll do it again this time, no matter what Peter says about her.

Only there are things she left behind on Tangier Island that she wanted to permanently forget; things she hoped would never see the light of day. It's going to take more fortitude than nearly anything else she's been through, but Sunday is going to show Peter who's the boss, and—surprise! It isn't him.

It was never him.

Rather than drinking the last sips of her wine, which she knows she doesn't need anyway, she flings the liquid toward the water and empties her glass, then turns and high steps through the soft sand all the way back to her house, determined to find a way to beat Peter at his own game.

Ruby

It's the last Friday night in September, and Ruby has decorated her house for fall. There are gourds and pumpkins on the mantel, the dining room table, and the kitchen counter. Vines of silk leaves in yellow, red, and orange are wound around the banisters of the steps in front of the house, where what looks like a hundred pumpkins in all sizes line the walkway, the steps, and the porch. Two tall cornstalks flank the front door, and pots of sunflowers are scattered amongst the Adirondack chairs, on the backs of which Ruby has artfully tossed lightweight plaid blankets for autumn evenings spent outdoors.

This is just such a night, as she's invited Sunday, Heather, and Marigold for drinks and appetizers, and she's spent the afternoon getting everything ready.

Harlow and Athena have decided to take a weekend trip to Destin together—their first trip off-island since arriving in the summer—and Ruby is excited for them to get their feet wet with a trip to the mainland, though she's still in no hurry to have Athena scuttle back to D.C. or for Harlow to head back to New York. Having her girls there has been blissful in a way that Ruby couldn't have anticipated, and watching Harlow go through therapy to slowly unwind herself after the terror of the bar shooting has been gratifying. Athena's heartbreak seems to be fading into the rearview mirror, and now it feels more like the three of them are living together by choice rather than out of fear and sadness, which Ruby dearly loves.

She's playing *Charlie Parker Live in Sweden 1950* on the speakers that are scattered around her house, and as Ruby rushes from pantry to kitchen, and from kitchen to laundry room to grab more linens, she hums along to the jazz music, stopping to check on the bacon-wrapped brussels sprouts and the fried mac and cheese balls in the oven. She's also got stuffed mushrooms, sweet chili chicken bites, and a veggie platter to make it seem less like they're filling their faces with snack food. But to be perfectly honest, Ruby loves nothing more than a party with hors d'oeuvres that she can gorge on and pretend that she "only had a few bites." She's also got the makings for hot buttered rum and for appletinis, and if everything goes as planned, Ruby will light her apple-cinnamon scented candles just in time to fill the house with fall goodness.

By six o'clock, she has everything set up the way she wants it, and she's even found the time to change out of her gray sweatsuit and into a pair of stretchy black jeans, an oversized cream-colored tunic, and a pair of brown suede ankle boots. Ruby pushes up her sleeves as the doorbell rings, and she turns down the music, which she's changed to a playlist that intentionally encompasses music of all genres and eras. "Domino" by Van Morrison is playing as Ruby throws open the front door with a smile to greet Heather, her first arrival.

"Hey!" Heather sweeps in, planting a kiss on Ruby's cheek. In her hands, she has a foil-covered platter, which she presents grandly. "I went old-school and made Rice Krispie treats," she says with a shrug. "They just sounded good."

"You can't go wrong," Ruby says, setting them on the island, which is already covered with the food she's spent the afternoon making. "Appletini?"

"Love one." Heather shrugs off her sweater and hangs it over the back of a tall bar chair, then climbs up and sits on it as she watches Ruby fix her martini. "This was such a fun idea. Thanks for inviting us all over."

For the most part, the women seem entirely used to the fact that they can count a former First Lady as one of their friends and as the hostess of their book club, but as Ruby watches Heather's eyes skim the framed photos of Ruby, Jack, and the girls on the side table in the living room, she can see the slightest hint of awe on her face.

Ruby smiles and turns her back to Heather as she works on the drinks, but she casts a glance over one shoulder. "Of course. I'm so happy you can all come, and I hope it's not too exclusive to just have the four of us, but Tilly and Vanessa are young, and I figured they might feel obligated to attend a little party with four old gals if their boss was asking, and we all know Molly likes to be in bed around seven, so...it's just us."

Heather uses both hands to toss her hair behind her shoulders before reaching out to take the martini glass that Ruby hands her. "Thank you. And no worries. The four of us is a perfect mix."

The doorbell rings again, and when Ruby opens the front door, Marigold is standing there in a body-hugging black catsuit, black suede, knee-high boots with a flat sole, and a loose, camel-colored cardigan that hangs off one shoulder. Her hair has been smoothed into a long sheet of light brown satin, and she's wearing makeup. She looks every inch the supermodel that she used to be, and Ruby takes a step back.

"Wowza. Are you just dropping by on your way to the catwalk?" Ruby accepts a kiss from Marigold as well as an expensive-looking box of macarons.

"Darling, the world is my catwalk," Marigold says in a faux British accent, letting her sweater fall off both shoulders alluringly as she stalks through the entryway, turning dramatically like she's at the end of the runway, then flinging herself around again and trotting off towards the kitchen.

Ruby laughs and starts to close the door when Sunday bounds up the stairs holding a mini crockpot in both hands.

"Don't close the door on me, girlfriend—I've got the corn and jalapeño dip!" Sunday is out of breath as she crosses the threshold. She kicks Ruby's front door shut behind her unceremoniously with her white Ked-clad foot. She's actually wearing a matching sweatsuit much like the one that Ruby had worn all day while getting the appetizers ready, but Ruby knows her friend well enough to know that Sunday won't care at all if she's walking into a room full of women dressed for a shindig while she's dressed for comfort. Since arriving on the island, Sunday has shed the formality of their previous life, opting instead for comfort and happiness, which Ruby wholly endorses.

Within ten minutes, everyone has cocktails in their hands, and they've each loaded a plate with appetizers and picked up one of the linen napkins that Ruby had ironed that very afternoon as she stood facing the windows looking out onto the beach.

"Let's sit outside," Ruby says, nodding at the door that leads to the wraparound deck. She's lit candles inside of heavy glass lanterns and set them on the railings, giving the porch a cozy feeling as the sun dips toward the horizon.

Sunday sits and spreads a plaid blanket over her lap right away, kicking off her tennis shoes and slipping her feet under her as she tucks into a pile of stuffed mushrooms and chicken bites.

Whoever designed the house had very thoughtfully installed speakers outside as well, so all Ruby has to do is hit a switch and the music spills out into the early fall evening, with Stevie Wonder singing "For Once In My Life" as the women get settled and put drinks on the arms of their chairs and rest their plates in their laps.

"This is amazing," Heather says, popping a fried mac and cheese ball into her mouth as she scans the beach happily. "I can see the ocean from the balcony of my townhouse, but it's nothing like having the waves crash just feet from where you're sitting. I bet you drink your coffee out here every morning and your wine here every evening, Ruby."

Ruby nods. "I definitely do. I realized pretty quickly that I could become numb to this kind of beauty, and I never want to take it for granted. Living here is a dream come true."

Sunday has chosen a hot buttered rum to drink, and she's sipping it quietly, looking out at the water.

"I've been here for almost ten years," Marigold says, crossing her legs and spreading a blanket over her lap. Her plate is heavy on the veggies and light on the fried appetizers, but she's got an appletini in her hand and she smiles wistfully. "And I never get tired of the ocean. I love not being recognized every time I walk out of my house, and I love that no one here asks me about what it was like to be married to Cobb Hartley. Every so often we have tourists and someone will approach me about all that stuff, but the people on Shipwreck Key know how to let a girl live a low-key life, and I respect that."

Finally, Sunday pipes up. "What *was* it like being married to a rockstar?"

Marigold laughs. "It was wild. And for the record, I don't mind talking about it at all with you guys—I just meant I hate going into a Starbucks and having the barista ask me whether Cobb kept his Grammys on our bookshelf." She sips her cocktail. "He kept them in the bathroom, by the way."

"I bet it's comparable to being married to a politician," Sunday says, ignoring the thought of Grammys on the bathroom counter. "People have expectations of who you *should* be, and it's easy for them to completely ignore who you actually are."

"I can second that," Ruby says, lifting her drink. The light from the candle flame catches the rim of her glass and Sunday looks her way. The women make eye contact and hold it meaningfully.

"Peter is going to tell all my secrets," Sunday says softly, still looking at Ruby. "He wants to save face politically, and I heard he's going to make me look like the bad guy in our divorce."

Ruby sets her glass on the arm of her chair and she sits forward, reaching for Sunday. She touches her arm. "No, Sun—no way can he do that."

Sunday nods vehemently. "He can, and he will. Trust me." She looks sad. "He'll drag me through the mud and come out smelling like a rose. It makes me sick."

"As it should," Heather says, sounding angry. "None of my ex-husbands are alive, but if they were, I'd like to think they wouldn't use anything they knew about my past against me."

"You'd be amazed what men will do when their political power is on the line," Sunday says, glancing Heather's way. "If you were never married to a man who doesn't mind treating you like an expendable resource, then you're a lucky woman."

Marigold's eyes flare as she shakes her head. "The public has no right to know your secrets or your past, Sunday, no matter what they try to make you think. You have to stop him. Can you get a legal injunction?"

Sunday gives a soft, disbelieving laugh. "No. It doesn't work like that. My only choice is to beat him to the punch somehow."

Heather crunches on a piece of cauliflower dipped in a creamy herb-ranch dressing. "Any idea how you'll do it?"

"I think the only way to win against your own past is to confront it head-on." Sunday holds her drink in both hands as she looks at the water. "I'm going to have to tell my own secrets before he does."

Ruby pulls a face; she knows what this will cost Sunday on a personal level, and she understands firsthand what it means to take a hard look at the parts of your life that you'd rather tuck away in the back of a closet.

"Sounds like we're sort of dealing with the same things," Ruby says to her friend. "And through my work with Dexter so far on the book, all I can say about it is that being forced to peel back the layers of your life —even the ugly ones—can be a little bit cathartic."

Sunday looks unconvinced. "There's stuff that I truly wanted to leave behind—I never wanted to talk about it with anyone. Not my kids, not myself, and certainly not the world at large. Don't we all have things like that in our pasts?"

Ruby, Heather, and Marigold all look lost in thought as they contemplate their own lives.

Heather is the first to break the silence. "I once took money from a church offering plate." The other women's heads all snap to attention. "I was nineteen and living in New York, trying to make it as a dancer, and I got kicked out of my apartment. I had nothing. I tried sleeping during the day in libraries or in the changing rooms at Macy's, but I could only do that for so long. So I was in this little church one day that looked like it had been there for centuries, and when no one was look-ing, I took a fistful of cash from the offering plate as it went by."

"Heather," Ruby says gently. "We all know that's technically 'wrong,' but what is the church if not a haven for those in need? You did what you had to do to survive, and if you believe in a higher power, then I think you can agree that you've been forgiven by now. You were just a kid, and it was purely out of survival."

Heather's eyes fill with tears. "Thank you for saying that. I never told a soul about it—none of my husbands, none of my friends, not my parents or siblings...no one. And I did go back to the church on a trip to the city with my second husband and I left a check that covers what I took by about fifty times over. I know I made my amends with that church, but I've never forgiven myself for doing it in the first place."

"Honey, you can forgive yourself now," Marigold says earnestly. She sets her plate on the railing in front of her and holds up both hands. "Listen to this, ladies. In the spirit of coming clean, I'm going to tell you the thing I most want to leave in my past." She takes a deep breath. "Once, when I was modeling and just getting started, I completely sabotaged another girl who was competing for the same job as me."

Sunday is staring at Marigold with her mouth open; Heather is waiting for someone to tell a secret more mortifying than the one she just revealed.

"It's true," Marigold goes on. "We were both about eighteen and living in Paris in what's called a 'model's apartment,' which is usually about four to six girls sharing a place to sleep, and we were up for the same campaign for a big shampoo company. The agency called and left a message that we were supposed to be at a certain place for the final casting, and I hid her portfolio under the towels in the bathroom and gave her the wrong address. I completely bombed her chances."

"Did you get the job?" Ruby asks, waiting eagerly for the outcome just like the other women.

"I most certainly did not," Marigold says, sounding prim. "And I didn't deserve to. It was one of the first times I truly experienced karma, and I can tell you that I got the message immediately. But regardless of me not getting the job, I've always felt terrible about it because *she* might have gotten it, and I ruined both of our chances for a gig that would have paid the bills for the better part of a year."

"Okay, that's pretty savage," Ruby says. "As for me, I think the worst thing I've done is to ignore Jack's mistress when she reached out to me. She tried to get to me through my lawyer, and she tried to get in touch by email, but I shut her down every time. It wasn't until she showed up at Marooned With a Book this summer that I realized I really should have just faced the music sooner." She stops talking for a minute, remembering Etienne Boucher and her twelve-year-old son, Julien, standing there in front of her. "I think that ignoring the fact that there were other human beings affected by Jack's choices was one of my bigger mistakes, and I'm not done paying that bill yet."

"How so?" Heather asks.

Ruby shrugs. "Our paths will cross again. When she gave me that letter that Jack had written, I was still ready to push her and her son out the door and be done with them for good, but that's not how it works. Her son and my daughters are siblings, whether I like it or not, and Etienne—that's her, and I rarely say her name out loud, so don't get too used to it—Etienne and I most likely have more unfinished business. I'm just not sure what it is yet."

Everyone looks at Sunday, waiting for her to unburden herself, should she feel like it. But instead of speaking, she picks up one of Heather's Rice Krispie treats and takes a big bite. They wait while she chews, licks the marshmallow from her thumb and forefinger, and looks at all of them.

"Well, the worst thing I've done is way worse than all of that combined," she says, wiping her hands on her linen napkin. "And I feel fairly certain that if you stick around, you'll hear all about it soon enough. If you can face your fears and talk to Dexter North about all of your dark stuff, Ruby, then I can go home to Tangier Island and deal with mine. So stay tuned, ladies. My turn is coming."

Marigold lifts her glass in the air in a toast. "You have my word," she says, "I'll stay tuned. And no matter what it is, I won't judge." She smiles at Sunday. "But if you ever try to steal one of my modeling jobs, I'll throw your portfolio in the Seine and send you on a wild goose chase around Paris."

Her joke lightens the mood just enough that the women collapse into a fit of laughter, but when Ruby glances at Sunday she sees that her friend is still troubled. It's going to take more than appetizers and cocktails and jokes to pull Sunday back from whatever is going on inside her heart, and Ruby knows exactly how she feels.

When the two women make eye contact again, Ruby gives her a private wink. They'll get through this together, just like they've gotten through so many other things.

Sunday

Dealing with Peter directly is a last resort. Sunday hasn't spoken to him since the last time she saw him, and any back and forth between them thus far has been handled via their attorneys.

But this is different. After the drinks and appetizers at Ruby's, she'd actually spent the night there, sleeping off the excess alcohol in Ruby's guest room and waking up to find that her friend had made bacon, eggs, and strong coffee to get them both over the hump of the morning following a night of drinking, talking, laughing, and crying.

"Call him," Ruby had said, setting a steaming mug in front of Sunday at the breakfast table. "Talk sense into him, Sun. You raised his children and stood by his side through a lot of crap, and he owes you way more than to simply keep his mouth shut about your past."

Sunday had huffed, her shoulders hunched as she sat there, inhaling the strong aroma of coffee and bacon.

"He'll do whatever he damn well pleases, and we both know that," she'd said, finally taking a fortifying sip of her coffee. "If he's got advisors telling him how things need to look to cast him in a favorable light, then he's going to listen to them, and not to me."

But Ruby had been insistent, and now here she is, sitting on her small deck with her phone in one hand. She taps the screen nervously with her thumbnail, squinting at the water instead of making the call.

Peter, she practices in her head, *I want you to cease and desist immediately with any discussion about my personal history.*

Peter, there is no way that you actually believe that I'm frigid, or that I alone caused the end of our marriage. And there's no way that anyone else will believe it either.

Listen, Bucko, you might be the former Vice President, but you have no right to drag me through the mud while you figure out your next move. Leave me alone, or I'll tell your daughters everything--and I mean EVERYTHING—that I know or that I saw with my own eyes. And I don't think you want that.

As Sunday mentally rehearses her speech, she chews on her bottom lip, imagining Peter laughing at any one of these proclamations. He would never kowtow to her or fold at even the hint of a threat from Sunday, but she knows that appealing to him as a father might work. It's a slim possibility, but one she's willing to lean on.

"Peter," she says as soon as he answers her call. "Don't hang up."

"Sunday, if I was just going to hang up on you, then I wouldn't have answered in the first place. I'm busy here, so start talking."

Sunday takes a deep breath and forges ahead. "I heard what you were planning to do, and I am not okay with you talking about my past in relation to our marriage. As a matter of fact, I'm not okay with you talking about our marriage, either, but I'm not sure if I can stop you."

Peter sighs, and it is the deep, world-weary sigh of a man who wants to let a woman know that she's already getting on his last nerve. "Listen, I may or may not do some interviews that involve a discussion of our life together. I'm not sure what exactly is being planned for the interviews, but I'll do whatever my advisors think is best."

"Peter," Sunday pleads. She knows she sounds like she's begging, but she can't help it--she is begging. "Let me get on with my life. Let me go. I gave you what you wanted. I raised your daughters, I stayed with you even though every person in Washington knew you were gay and sleeping around--"

Peter clears his throat angrily here. "This isn't a secure line, Sunday. I don't want you using words that label me as anything inflammatory, and

I won't admit to doing anything that might come back to bite me in the ass."

"Fine. While you were out scouring dark, seedy bars for new constituents who prefer to vote with their pants down, I was at home raising your kids."

"They're technically not mine, Sunday."

His words make her blood run cold. She knows that a part of Peter's desire to adopt had been to create a visual of himself as a happy family man, and also to do something that people might view as big-hearted and charitable, but she'd always believed that, deep down, Peter loved being a father to Olive and Cameron and that he felt as she did: that the universe brought them the right girls; that somehow a higher power had known that these were *their* children. In fact, she still believes that he feels this way, but Peter knows exactly what to say to hit Sunday where it hurts.

"I'm speechless," Sunday says, standing up from where she's been sitting on her little deck. She walks over to the railing and stares at the powdery sand without really seeing it. "The fact that you would even say that is beyond messed up, Peter. It's deranged. I'm so disgusted by you right now, even if you are just saying things you don't mean to try and get under my skin."

Peter sighs again. "Listen, honey, you and I are never going to see eye to eye on this, and that's okay. Men and women are just wired differently."

"We're wired differently when it comes to loving our own children?"

Sunday can almost see him shrugging on his end of the call. "Not necessarily. But I did my job: I provided for them and gave them an amazing life and a fascinating childhood. Now they're adults and they're free to go out and conquer the world. They don't need me. They don't even call me. So mazel tov, kids."

"Olive calls you," Sunday counters angrily. "She was down here a couple of weeks ago, and she told me all the things you two had talked about last time she called."

"Fine. So Olive calls occasionally and needs money for her bakery." Peter sounds bored. "And because I'm her father, I feel obligated to help her out. Is that what you're looking for? An admission that I'm their father?"

Sunday shakes her head even though Peter can't see her. "No. That's not it at all. I *know* you're their father, but sometimes I'm not sure that you do. For years you've put politics first, then family."

"Cameron never deigns to call--not even for money."

"Can you blame her? Thanks to you, she won't call me either. She thinks I stayed too long, and she lost all respect for me as a woman."

"Feminism is destroying the world," Peter says, sounding annoyed.

"*Men* are destroying the world. How many wars can you name that have been started by women?"

"I'm sure the truth lies somewhere in between, but listen, Sun, I need to cut you off here. I've got a meeting to attend, and we're just talking in circles here."

"Do not speak about me in your interviews, Peter. I will not stand for it."

"Then sit down for it, because if our marriage comes up, I'll say whatever I need to say. Take care, Sunday." Peter ends the call.

Sunday is so angry that she wants to throw her phone. She wants to stomp and kick things and throw a framed wedding photo of herself and Peter against a wall and watch it shatter, but of course she no longer has any framed wedding photos of them. Her frustration is so out of control, so massive, that she doesn't even know how to begin to manage it. So instead of doing anything destructive, she looks up and down the beach, sees no one, and pulls her dress over her head, tossing it onto a deck chair. She's standing there in just her lingerie, and without thinking, she steps out of her underwear and unhooks her bra, tossing it on top of the dress.

Without giving it a second thought, Sunday runs straight across the sand to the water, and she doesn't slow down as she begins to splash through the waves, feeling the cool surf as it envelops her naked body. Once she's covered to the waist, she falls into it, using her arms to swim forward as the water cascades over her back and caresses her skin.

She is weightless. She is not Peter Bond's soon-to-be ex-wife. She is not a woman whose older daughter refuses to take her calls. She is not a woman who has secrets that she wants to keep in her past. She is a woman with her whole life ahead of her and the freedom to choose how to live it. She is a woman who owns a house with sand and sky and beach and--

"Ma'am?" a man's voice calls out.

Sunday turns her head in surprise, glancing over one bare shoulder at the water's edge, where Banks, Ruby's Secret Service agent, stands with his hands on his hips and sweat dripping from his hairline.

Oh god.

Sunday is a woman stuck in the ocean with no clothes.

Sunday is naked.

"Hi!" She waves, attempting to sound cheery and unbothered. "Gorgeous day, isn't it?"

Banks frowns into the sun and then looks back at Sunday. "It is. But these are some pretty good-sized waves, and there's a strong rip current right here."

It's Sunday's turn to frown; no one had warned her that she was living on a beach with a massive rip current, and she hasn't been in the water until now, which is amazing to her, given the fact that she's lived there for three months already.

"I'll be fine!" she shouts back, smiling to put him at ease.

"Actually, I'll just hang out here and wait for you to finish your swim, if you don't mind." Banks hooks a thumb over his shoulder at her house. "I can stretch out after my run right there on your porch and be within shouting distance. It would be wrong for me to leave you here alone, Mrs. Bond."

Ignoring the fact that her nakedness is by far her most pressing issue, Sunday feels indignation well up inside of her. "No more 'Mrs. Bond,' please. Or 'ma'am.' I want to be Sunday from this point forward when we see each other, okay?"

Her voice carries across the waves between them. Banks, hands still firmly on hips, nods. "Okay. As you wish."

A smile plays at Sunday's lips as she treads water, feeling the cool fingers of it touching the parts of her that no one has touched in ages. "Thank you," she says. "That's better."

"Then, Sunday, I'll be right there until you're safely out of the water," Banks says, tipping his head at the steps that lead down from her porch to the sand.

Sunday freezes; her legs and arms stop moving and she momentarily dips into the water, getting some in her mouth. She splutters and begins to tread water again.

"Actually, Banks, there's a very small situation happening here that might make you uncomfortable." Sunday attempts to toss her hair the way she might on dry land, trying to give the impression that she hasn't a care in the world. "As it turns out, I'm here in the water...naked. And I have no towel."

The look on Banks's face morphs from one of concern when he hears the words "small situation," to a look of sheer, unbridled amusement. He smothers a laugh. "You think a naked woman is a situation I'm uncomfortable with?" he calls out, his voice full of mirth.

Sunday rolls her eyes. "Listen, if I come out of this water, you will not be able to un-see that vision, and it's not like anyone's ever going to make me the centerfold of the *Sports Illustrated Swimsuit Issue.*"

"Their loss," Banks says with what looks like a wink, but could possibly have just been a grain of sand in his eye.

Sunday stays there, treading water. "Look, I know we're on a first name basis now--at least, you are with me. What's your first name, anyway? And how do I not already know it?" She frowns as she thinks of the years she's known Banks but yet somehow still knows nothing about him.

"It's Henry," he says, still smiling. "But never Hank."

Sunday nearly chokes on water again as she laughs. "Hank Banks? Yeah, that would be terrible. Didn't your parents consider that when they named you?"

Banks shrugs. "Probably not. And most people don't even try it, but I like to shut it down before it gets going."

Sunday eyes his impressively developed upper body, which is once again not covered by a shirt as he takes his run on the beach, and imagines that most people probably *don't* mess with Henry Banks. "Understood," she says, sinking a bit further so that the water is up to her chin. "But I'm still not coming out of the water while you're here."

"Where's your towel?"

Sunday screws up her face like she's in pain. "Actually, I hadn't planned to come into the water...like this. Or at all. So I just tossed my clothes on the deck and ran out here. It was kind of on a whim." She feels her face redden at the image of Banks walking up onto her deck and seeing the underwear she'd simply kicked off and the bra she'd flung onto the chair. She feels that more explanation might be necessary, so she gives a good kick and pulls herself forward through the water with her arms, coming a few feet closer to him. "I was on a phone call with my husband, and it just...filled me with rage. I didn't know what to do besides break stuff, so I ended up out here. There's no other good explanation for it."

Banks holds up a hand. "Please--I've gone through a divorce. Say no more. Where can I find a towel for you? And may I go inside your house to get it?"

"Of course," Sunday says, charmed by how formal the man is when she's as naked as the day she was born and swimming in the ocean in broad daylight. "And there's a linen closet in the hallway right next to the downstairs bathroom. There are plenty of towels there."

"Stay where you are, please," Banks says, turning towards her house. "I don't like leaving you out here alone at all, but I'll be as fast as I possibly can."

True to his word, Banks runs across the sand and up the steps to her house, disappears inside, and is back to the edge of the water in less than sixty seconds. Or what must be less than sixty seconds, as Sunday has no watch on, and she isn't really counting. But either way, she's amused at his concern for her safety, and appreciative for the towel, which he sets on the sand and then backs away from like it's a bomb that might detonate at any second.

"I'm going to turn my back," Banks calls out. "So don't worry about me seeing anything."

Sunday smirks as she steps out of the water, stealing another glance up and down the beach to make sure no one else is around. When she's sure she's in the clear, she runs to the edge of the water, breasts held in her arms for modesty, and snatches the towel from the sand, wrapping it around her body and tucking it tightly like she's just stepped out of the shower.

"There," she says breathlessly, wiping the wet strands of her hair from her eyes. "Better. Thank you."

Banks turns around slowly and then smiles, satisfied that Sunday is safe from the rip tide. "Just out of curiosity, what was your plan for getting back to your clothing, if I might be so bold as to inquire?"

Sunday tries for insouciance as she shrugs one sun-kissed shoulder. "I probably would have just held my head high and walked my buns across the sand like I didn't have a care in the world."

Banks gives a gravelly laugh that sounds like it's full of dark and inappropriate thoughts. "Well, then I guess I have your almost-ex-husband to thank for pissing you off royally, don't I?" He lifts one eyebrow at her and then turns and picks up his run along the shoreline like nothing has happened.

Sunday doesn't even pretend not to stare at his muscled back and strong calves as he disappears down the beach.

Sunday

~~~

There's no way that Sunday can sleep and dream and not conjure images of Banks on the beach, half-naked himself in her mind's eye as she emerges from the water, slick and wet and sun-dappled like a mermaid. Each time she dreams about it the outcome is slightly different, but always he gives her looks of longing, appreciation, and lust, and she wakes up feeling short of breath.

Can anyone blame a woman so starved for romantic feeling? Is it possible to hold it against a woman in her sexual prime, a woman inhabiting a body that might not be exactly what it once was, but one that is so familiar to her that she knows exactly what to do with it should she ever get the opportunity? Certainly no one could misunderstand her need to take an interaction like the one Sunday and Banks had on the beach and try it on over and over again, breaking it in like a favorite pair of jeans.

Ruby catches Sunday doing exactly this as they stroll down Seadog Lane together one afternoon.

"You look like the cat that got the canary," Ruby says, watching her curiously.

"Not yet. But the canary is perched on my windowsill every morning, so sooner or later I'll catch him."

"Spill." Ruby pulls open the door to Doubloons and Full Moons, the tiny shop sandwiched between The Scuttlebutt and Chips Ahoy, where everyone gets their coffee and their fish and chips, respectively.

The bell over the door tinkles lightly and they walk into the dim, air-conditioned shop. Ella, the owner of Doubloons and Full Moons, gives them a little wave from the corner of the store, where she's showing someone a deck of tarot cards. Doubloons and Full Moons is full of fabulous beaded and handmade jewelry sourced from all over the world, but it's also the island's own metaphysical shop, and Ella does a brisk business in tarot card, palm, tea leaf, and psychic readings. Ruby waves back and leads Sunday over to a rack of long, beaded necklaces from Africa.

"There's nothing to spill," Sunday says, trying to sound casual as she selects a long, turquoise and coral beaded necklace from a rack and holds it up to her collarbone. She looks into the mirror that Ella has hanging on one wall. "Do you like this?"

"I think you look amazing in anything, Sun. You pull off every color and every style you try, and I'm not just saying that."

Sunday puts the necklace back. "I think you're just buttering me up so I'll dish some dirt."

Ruby picks up a silver bracelet with a square opal inlaid on its wide band. "I speak the truth, but I definitely want to hear what's up."

"Okay, I guess I can't keep it from you forever anyway, and I also can't wait to see your face."

Ruby sets down the bracelet and turns to Sunday. "I'm intrigued."

"Well...last week I finally called Peter."

"Ugh. You should have told me, Sun! I would have brought over a bottle of wine afterwards so we could slog through all the feelings—I'm sure that call brought up plenty."

"I actually slogged through those feelings by stripping off my clothes in the middle of the day and running into the water naked."

Ruby's eyes go wide with disbelief. She cackles and then catches herself, putting a hand over her mouth and glancing over at Ella and her customer. "Sunday Bellows Bond!" she says in a loud whisper. "You ran your bare, white bum out into the water where anyone could see?"

"I absolutely did, and it wasn't 'anyone' who saw me...it was Banks."

49

Sunday cringes as she waits for Ruby's response, which turns out to be another cackle—only this time she doesn't stifle it.

"I'm beside myself here," Ruby says, laughing even harder. "But I'm also kind of curious what happened next."

"He told me he couldn't leave me in the water alone because of a rip tide, and then he ran into my house and got me a towel so I didn't have to flash my butt at the world."

"Thank god for that," Ruby says, holding her stomach as she catches her breath from laughing.

"Yeah." Sunday turns back to a rack of necklaces and picks out one with little sterling silver butterflies dangling from it. "But now I can't stop thinking about being on the beach naked with Banks. That's not weird, is it?" she confesses, wincing as she waits for Ruby's judgment to kick in.

"Nah, definitely not weird. An extremely attractive man saw you in the water naked—I'm assuming he was out for a jog, which means no shirt?"

"Yeah, and I've watched him run by my house before," Sunday says, feeling guilty.

"I doubt you're the only woman on the island who enjoys the scenery whenever Henry Banks is around. I mean, come on: square jaw, firm body, broad shoulders, quiet and mysterious...you're fifty-four, not dead. No one expects you not to entertain a little harmless fantasy about a guy like that."

"Wait, does that mean you have a thing for Banks?" Sunday asks, trying to sound nonchalant as she inspects the butterfly necklace and tries to imagine it on Olive.

"God, no. Definitely no." Ruby puts both hands in the air like she's surrendering in a bank heist. "He's handsome, yes, but I respect his job, what he does for me, and the fact that he does it so well. I would never want to get those wires crossed, and furthermore, I'm just not attracted to him like that. We've known each other for so long."

"You're not attracted to him?" Sunday looks at her like she's crazy.

"Nah. Banks is cool as a cucumber and a damn good Secret Service agent, but I've always been into guys who are more cerebral—you know, the ones who can sit around and talk about books and who get excited about things like a perfect sunset, or the way a smell reminds them of something important."

"And you know a lot of men who are into sunsets and the memories invoked by scents?" Sunday leans a hip against the counter that holds all the necklace racks. "Ohhh, wait. I feel like Mr. Dexter North might be into books. And, oh, heyyyy—he's a writer, so he's probably pretty adept at using his senses and appreciating the magic of the natural world." She sweeps her hands through the air dramatically, sounding just as jokingly sarcastic as she looks.

Ruby's cheeks turn pink and she tucks her hair behind her ears. "We're just working together on a project."

"Uh huh. And I'm just thinking of doing friendly things with Banks, like trading one-person dinner recipes, or discussing the fastest way to get to the mainland."

Ruby glances around and lowers her voice again. "But Sun, he's *way* younger than me."

"Not this again. Give me a break—the man is a man, and you're a gorgeous, successful woman in your own right. So take the credit you deserve, and accept that he might be attracted to you in spite of the fact that you're fast approaching the big five-oh."

Ruby makes a gagging face. "Fifty."

"Hey, don't knock it. Not everyone makes it to fifty, and most don't make it there with as much panache as you."

"Thank you. And you're right," Ruby says. "I'm here, I have my health, and I have two great kids. I shouldn't be worrying myself about a few crow's feet or some gray hairs."

"You most definitely should not," Sunday says, taking Ruby by the elbow and steering her towards Ella now that the other customer has picked her pack of tarot cards, paid for them, and left the shop.

"Ladies," Ella says, spreading her arms expansively. She's wearing an ombre shirt of yellows, oranges, and pinks, and as she lifts her arms, the fabric flows all around her like she's got batwings. Ella has a gold ring on each finger of both hands, and she wears her long, graying hair pulled into a chic topknot, with just a touch of bright lipstick to finish off her look. "Welcome, welcome, welcome," Ella says, clapping her hands together and lacing all of her fingers so that her rings clink together. "You're here for a reading." It's not a question.

"I—" Ruby is shaking her head no, but Sunday grabs her hand to silence her.

"Yes, we are," Sunday says. "We heard great things about your readings, and I really wanted to try. Ruby is along for the ride, but she might want one too."

Ruby looks surprised, but says nothing.

Ella squints at both of them. "Sunday," she says, looking directly at Sunday. They've met around the island a number of times, but Sunday wouldn't have flinched if a woman she'd never met had greeted her by name; it certainly wouldn't be the first time. "I feel that you need a psychic reading. You and me, sitting in my room, and me channeling all of the messages that you need to hear. Does that sound right?"

Sunday nods. "It sounds perfect. I'm ready for all of the messages."

Ruby holds her purse across the front of her body protectively as she watches Sunday. They know each other well enough that Sunday knows Ruby isn't fundamentally opposed to the psychic reading, she's just not totally convinced yet that it's for her.

"Listen," Ruby says, "I'm going to grab a coffee next door and chat with Molly. You let me know when you're done and then we can see how the rest of the afternoon looks for us time-wise." She shoots Sunday a meaningful look.

Ruby leaves and the bells on the door tinkle behind her. Sunday waits while Ella locks the front door of the shop and turns the sign over to the "Be Back Soon!" side.

"Follow me, darling," Ella says, sweeping through the shop with her batwing shirt drifting around her.

Ella's room is in the back of the building, and it's nothing more than an eight-by-eight square foot space that's been partitioned off from the rest of Doubloons and Full Moons. She pulls a curtain aside for Sunday and motions for her to choose one of the two comfortable looking stuffed chairs. Sunday sits in a yellow corduroy chair and puts a decorative pillow in her lap so that she can run her fingers through its tassels as she listens to whatever Ella is about to tell her.

With a quick flick of her wrist, Ella strikes a match and lights a candle on a tiny shelf that's tucked into the corner of the room. She waves a hand over it to disperse the scent around the room.

"Patchouli and plum blossom," Ella says, sinking into the other chair, which is covered in a brocade fabric that's been worn down over years of use. "Now," she says, folding her hands together in her lap. "We have things to discuss."

Sunday takes a deep breath and nods. "Yes, we do."

With her eyes closed, Ella breathes in and out, slower and slower until Sunday isn't sure whether the woman is asleep or just meditating. Finally, as if in a trance, Ella speaks. "There's water in your past."

Sunday thinks of her life on Tangier Island, which was totally dependent on water: on the tides, on the fish her father and grandfather could catch, on the way the waves swallowed up her brother and left her family bereft. "Yes, there was water," she says.

Ella nods. "The water gives and the water takes," she says, the words coming from her in a tone that's devoid of any hills and valleys. It's as if the words are flowing out without her even knowing what she's saying. "And you didn't want it to take you, so you left."

"Yes." Sunday's voice is a whisper. "I left."

"But you need to revisit this past—at least once more. There's no way to escape it."

Sunday inhales sharply through her nose, nodding though Ella's eyes are still closed and she can't see her.

"You have children." Again, this is a statement, not a question. "One won't speak to you." Ella's brow pulls into a frown and she looks like she's watching a movie on the inside of her eyelids as her eyes move around furiously beneath the lids. "There is anger there, and misunderstanding. She doesn't know you, Sunday. Neither of your children knows the real you."

Sunday is nodding silently as her eyes fill with tears. Ella is right, of course, and she seems to know that Sunday has two kids—although she realizes that there's still a chance that Ella simply knows those details because everyone knows them—but Ella is soft by nature and both ethereal and gentle; there's nothing about her that screams "huckster."

"That's true," Sunday agrees, trying not to give in to the sensation of needing to say more or to expand on Ella's statements. "They don't truly know me."

Ella's eyes open slowly. "They need to know you, Sunday—they deserve to know you. You need to show them where you come from and explain who you are so that no one else tells your story for you."

The hair on Sunday's arms stands up as goosebumps rise all over her body. This is *precisely* what's about to happen, and there's no way that Ella could have ever known that. No way at all.

"So, you think I need to take my children home with me?"

Ella lifts both shoulders and lets her head fall to one side as she ponders the question. "Well, that would be one way, I suppose. Show them exactly where your roots are planted, because we never fully yank our roots from the soil, no matter how far from home we go. We can try, but there's always a part of us that's bound to our beginnings. And some of us leave bits behind that we can never recover. It's time for you to go back and try to recapture those parts of yourself. This trip will be all about acceptance and letting go."

Now Sunday has gone beyond just watery eyes and chills; she has started to cry—to sob, really—and she puts both hands to her face to hide behind them.

"Sunday, Sunday," Ella says, reaching out with both of her hands and putting them on Sunday's knees. She applies a bit of pressure, bringing Sunday back to the moment. "I know it's emotional to set down the baggage we carry everywhere, but set it down, honey. Set it down for a minute, and let yourself cry if you need to."

So that's exactly what Sunday does: she lets herself cry in the tiny back room of Doubloons and Full Moons while Ella waits patiently, watching her and nodding with encouragement.

"I don't normally revisit any of this," Sunday explains through her tears, swiping at her cheeks. "I left my childhood and my adolescence behind, and I never went back. It's so hard to go back."

"It is," Ella agrees. "Particularly when conventional wisdom tells us that we must never look back, always forward. But that's not necessarily true. In order to grow, we need to reconcile the past and who we used to be with our present and who we have become. So go home and do that, but do it *with* your children. It will serve all of you well."

"I just...you're so right—about all of this." Sunday digs in her purse for a packet of Kleenex, but Ella reaches over to where the candle is flickering and pulls a box from a shelf beneath it. "Thank you." Sunday pulls out two tissues from the box and wipes at her eyes and nose. "My past has been coming back lately, and I don't think I can ignore it anymore, so I think I'm headed back to Tangier Island. Thank you."

Ella's eyebrows lift in surprise. "Off the coast of Virginia? Where the older locals still speak with a faintly British accent?"

Sunday nods. "Yep, that's the place. It's a tiny fishing village suspended in time. Very insulated against progress, and full of secrets."

Ella gives her a knowing look and leans forward, putting just her fingertips on Sunday's left knee this time as she stares into her eyes. "Then you go back there, and you look those secrets in the face and put them to bed once and for all. And no matter what happens, don't let *anyone else* bury you under the weight of your own past."

* * *

Sunday emerges from Doubloons and Full Moons clutching a tissue and shaking as she dabs at her eyes.

"Oh my god, Sun!" Ruby rushes up to her, holding an iced coffee from The Scuttlebutt in one hand, and her phone in the other. "What happened?" She casts a glance at the front of the shop, looking like she's ready to go in and confront Ella about whatever she might have said to get Sunday so worked up. "Are you okay?"

Sunday nods and loops her arm through Ruby's, and as she does, Ruby's phone buzzes in her hand.

"I'm fine," Sunday sniffs. "Do you need to get that?"

"No, no," Ruby says, shaking her head and brushing the call off. "I'll deal with everything else later. What the hell happened in there? Did she freak you out? Tell you something bad? I wasn't sure how I felt about this whole fortune telling business in the first place, but now I'm sure it's bad news. Look at you, Sun!"

"I'm okay—I promise. It was actually really good. Ignore the tears, because they're cathartic."

Ruby looks unconvinced, but steers Sunday to a little wrought iron bistro table outside of The Scuttlebutt and forces her to sit. "Tell me what happened."

Sunday reaches for Ruby's iced coffee and takes a long pull from the straw before settling in. "Okay, so she knew right away that I have two kids—"

"Everyone knows that," Ruby counters, looking dubious. "You're an extremely public figure."

"Wait, there's more. She knew that I'm not on speaking terms with one of my kids, and she knew that I came from somewhere that relies entirely on water."

"Tangier Island," Ruby says softly, nodding.

"Exactly. And she said she knew that someone was going to use my past against me, or tell my tale...or something. And that basically I need to go back there with my girls and let them know who I *truly* am. Because I've never done that. They don't really know anything about my past."

Ruby is watching her face and listening intently. "So you're going to take Olive and Cam back to Tangier with you?"

Sunday blows out a long breath through pursed lips, making her cheeks look like a puffer fish. "Well, I'm going to ask them to come. I can't make them do anything—they're grown women. But I hope they'll want to." She turns her head so that she's looking out at the water, which is glittering in the midday sun. "I guess if I had the chance to go back to where my mom was from and to learn what had made her the way she was, I'd want to take it."

"But that's from the perspective of a woman in her mid-fifties who knows the value of that opportunity. Olive and Cam might not be able to see yet how important this is—for you *or* for them."

"That's true," Sunday says, looking forlorn. "But all I can do is ask. I can make all the travel plans, pay for the trip, and keep my fingers crossed that they'll come."

Ruby intertwines her right hand with Sunday's left one from across the little table and looks her in the eyes. "Well, all I can say is that I think it's incredibly brave, Sun. Peter hasn't left you with much of a choice in the matter, but even without him being a pain in the ass, it takes courage to unpack things that haven't seen the light of day in a while. I'm behind you all the way."

Sunday picks up the iced coffee from the table, wrapping her hand around the cold condensation that's dripping down the outside of the cup. "Some of these things haven't seen the light of day *ever*," she says, sipping Ruby's cold coffee again. "But Ella told me not to let anyone else bury me under the weight of my own past, and come hell or high water, I'm gonna make sure no one does."

Ruby

Ruby has checked into the Conrad Downtown in Manhattan with Banks in tow, and is unpacking her toiletries and filling the drawers of the dresser with her satin underthings and all of her foldable clothes as she thinks about Sunday. Ruby had left for New York City and her meeting with Dexter North on a Tuesday morning, but had made Sunday promise to tell her everything about her upcoming trip to Tangier Island. So far Sunday has only been able to get Olive to agree to the trip, but she and Olive are both working on Cameron, and with any luck at all, they'll fly to Virginia and take the ferry to the island together before the end of the week. Ruby has her fingers crossed that it works out, as she knows how much it means to Sunday to confront the things that haunt her from her past, and to do it all with her girls at her side so that she can hopefully heal the rift that's grown between her and Cameron.

Her cell phone dings on the bed as she walks across her hotel room in the white slippers that were sitting beneath a fluffy white robe that's hanging from a hook next to the glass-enclosed rain shower.

The message is from Dexter: *You made it! I'm finishing a meeting here. What time should we plan to see one another?*

She stares at the screen, reading and re-reading his message as she tries to decipher his meaning. He said "plan to see one another" when he could have just as easily said "meet up" or "get together and start talking." But maybe she's splitting hairs when she doesn't need to be. It's entirely possible that Dexter simply typed whatever came to mind first, and that he had no intention of stressing the fact that they're about to see one another again in person.

Any time is good for me--I have no other plans for this trip but to see you. She hits send before overthinking how much this sounds like she's flown up to New York to go on a date with Dexter North. And in truth she *should* ask to meet Ursula, her Manhattan-based virtual assistant, for a cup of coffee or to take her to lunch, but she thinks it's also fine not to. She and Ursula have a warm working relationship, but she knows that them meeting face-to-face isn't an imperative, nor is it expected.

Therefore this trip *is* about seeing Dexter and working on their book together. *His book*, Ruby reminds herself, *not "our" book.*

She's about to drop her phone on the bed and go back to unpacking her belongings for her four-day stay when it dings again.

How about if I message you when I'm in a cab coming your direction. I'll meet you in the lobby and we can do a late lunch at a place I know.

I'll be here, Ruby types, then sets her phone down again.

She walks to the window of the hotel and looks at the street below, watching as people travel to and from work, into and out of stores and cafes, living their lives and doing the things that people do. Ruby loves New York--the energy, the nightlife, the culture of a city where people come to get things done. New York is not a city built for mere survival, and the thing she loves most about being there is the current of electricity that runs through everything: the traffic, the subway screaming in and out of the stations, the people crossing the streets between honks and shouts from cab drivers, the theaters, concerts, and art galleries--all of it thrums with life.

Ruby pulls a chair and a table over to the window and for the next two hours, she sits with a cup of coffee that she brews in the little Keurig on the dresser. Between chapters of the book that she's reading for book club, she watches the slice of sky between the buildings across the street and casts glances at the humanity teeming below on the ground.

She's lost in thought when her phone pings again: *Be there in ten minutes. Meet in the lobby?*

Ruby stands and slips her feet into the ankle boots she's brought with her. She feels a thrill at the prospect of a bright blue fall afternoon spent outside on the streets of the city, and all of a sudden, she's hungry, too.

On my way down, she writes. *See you soon!*

* * *

The place Dexter knows is a Mediterranean restaurant on Broadway with gorgeous outdoor seating. He's already made a reservation, so they're shown right to a table for two, and he offers Ruby the banquette--a green leather seat that faces the sidewalk--and he takes the woven wicker chair with a marble table between them. Banks sits about twenty feet away in a chair with his back against the building so that he's facing Ruby and Dexter. He's wearing sunglasses and scanning the crowd and assessing the situation, just as he always does.

"Here you are," the hostess says, handing them each a menu. "Your server will be right over."

By the time they're ready to order, Ruby and Dexter have decided on the hummus plate to start, and then a chicken schnitzel and a pan-seared salmon with chickpeas. Their waiter suggests a bottle of champagne that Ruby sees is a hundred and fifty-five dollars; Dexter agrees without flinching.

"I'm expensing everything," he says, handing both of their menus to the waiter and leaning his elbows on the table as he looks at Ruby. "So go wild while we're here, got it?"

Ruby laughs, feeling her spirits lighten as three pigeons peck around near the tables, picking up fallen french fries and bits of flatbread. As she'd hoped, the trees along Broadway are on fire with autumn, and everywhere she looks, women are wrapped in cashmere shawls, chunky sweaters, and the kind of lightweight scarves that are more for show than for warmth. Fall has arrived on the back of a crisp, beautiful day, and New Yorkers are making the most of it.

"Did you decide what you wanted to do here that was fun?" Dexter asks, still watching Ruby across the table like she's the only other person on the planet. In truth, the banquette runs the length of the sidewalk outside the restaurant, and at every table there are people of interest: women with tattoos on their arms, men with cleanly shaped beards, little dogs on leashes sitting obediently beneath the chairs of their masters. So many people and sounds mixed together feels like sensory overload for Ruby after six months on Shipwreck Key, and she's taking it all in like it's a feast for the eyes.

"Well, with weather this beautiful, I think a walk through Central Park is a must."

"Or a carriage ride?" Dexter offers. "I could take notes easier if we were sitting and talking."

Ruby laughs again, watching as the waiter approaches and uncorks the champagne for them. "Ever practical," she says, lifting her champagne flute to toast Dexter. He raises his glass and holds it to hers. "Cheers," Ruby says, "to teamwork. And to talk therapy, which is sometimes what I feel like I'm doing when I talk to you."

Dexter looks amused as he takes a drink of his champagne and sets it on the table. "Oh? I come across like a therapist? I mean, I guess I can see why, given that I'm asking leading questions and prying into your inner life. But then I guess I should ask: is it helping? In any way at all?"

It's Ruby's turn to put her elbows on the table and look at him. "Yeah, weirdly, I think it is. There are times when I don't want to talk about something, but when that happens I look at *why* I don't want to examine it, then I convince myself to just try it. I give myself permission to tell you to move on if it becomes physically uncomfortable--"

"Like heart palpitations?"

"Like my stomach hurts, or yeah, my heart races--but that usually doesn't happen. It's almost like forcing yourself to go numb through exposure, you know? The more you talk about something, the less it hurts."

"I see." Dexter glances at the greenery that lines the shelf above the banquette behind Ruby. She knows it's filled with potted plants and flowers, and that overhead are hanging chandeliers in a variety of colors that are anchored to the outdoor structure, but she doesn't tear her eyes away from Dexter's handsome face. He looks back at her. "Then let's try something new. Rather than me opening with a question that's been on my mind, I'm going to ask you to think of something: a story, an anecdote--anything, really--and tell it to me."

"Now?" Ruby glances up at the waiter as he sets down their hummus tray. She picks up a piece of flatbread and dips it into the olive oil on the platter. "Over lunch?"

"Yeah. I say let's start strong. I want this trip to be a combination of great food, Central Park, and anything else you want to do mixed in with us talking about anything you'd like to talk about."

"Ah," Ruby says, taking a bite of her flat bread as she watches the pigeons scampering in her direction at the possibility of potential snacks being dropped to the ground. "This feels like a new therapy tactic."

"More like a biographer tactic," Dexter admits, cocking his head to one side as he reaches for a piece of bread and dips it in hummus. "Actually, in all honesty, I'm just winging it with you most of the time, Ruby. I've definitely gone into interviews with agendas and goals, and with the understanding that I was taking on a serious project, but I'm being truthful with you when I say that this is more like having a conversation with a real person than grilling someone whose life I want to turn inside out on the page."

"Oh, good," Ruby says with an amused laugh. "I'm so glad you aren't just looking to rip up my life and regurgitate it on paper for the masses."

Dexter holds up both hands. "Hey, my work sometimes requires a little regurgitation."

"So this first conversation can be about anything I want?"

"Anything," Dexter says, drinking more champagne. "It's the lady's choice."

Ruby thinks about this, looking at a table through the window where two women who appear to be in their eighties are laughing uproariously and sharing a bottle of red wine. One of them is wearing a silk scarf tied jauntily around her neck, and the other is in a denim jacket that's covered in all kinds of colorful patches—rock bands, a smiley face, a glittery rainbow, and flowers.

Dexter is waiting patiently as Ruby thinks of a topic. He tops off their champagne glasses, but says nothing as she thinks.

"I've got it." Ruby smiles at him with satisfaction as the waiter drops off their salmon and schnitzel. She waits until he's offered them fresh ground pepper and vanished again before she goes on. "I want to talk about the best year of your life."

Dexter frowns like he's confused. "The best year of *my* life? Why?"

"Yeah. I want to hear how old you were, what was so great about it, and what you learned from that year." Ruby picks up her flatware. "And why? I guess I would answer that with *why not*?"

Dexter's face relaxes and he picks up his fork. "Okay, that's a fair question, and a creative one, which is a high compliment from someone whose job it is to come up with creative questions."

Ruby adjusts the gray linen napkin on her lap. She's ready to be the recipient of someone else's life stories for a few minutes.

"Okay," Dexter says, gazing up at the wooden beams of the outdoor structure above them. "The best year of my life was 2003. I was sixteen." Ruby makes a disbelieving sound as she looks up from her chicken; this makes Dexter smile. "I've already done the math: I know you were twenty-nine that year, which highlights the fact that we're from entirely different generations. You were raising kids in 2003, and I was listening to Outkast and getting my driver's license."

Ruby shakes her head. Thirteen years suddenly seems like a lot, except that Dexter has the professional and life experience of someone much older, which gives him a world-weary look that only adds to his appeal.

"Yes, I had two young girls and a husband who was already looking ahead to a run for the Oval Office," Ruby says, then bites her tongue; she wants this to be about Dexter, not about her. "But go on."

"So the summer I was sixteen I had been working for three years at my uncle's auto parts store, and I bought a 1957 Ford Fairlane that needed a ton of work."

Ruby gives a low whistle. "Nice choice. A classic."

"Absolutely. I worked on it every waking second, and I had it running and sounding good, but it needed a fresh coat of paint. I wanted it to be white and cherry red."

Ruby picks up her flute and drinks a bit of bubbly as Dexter goes on with a faraway look in his eyes.

"I needed about eight hundred dollars more to paint that car, and my uncle had promised me as much overtime as he could give me without getting flagged for some sort of infraction for overworking a minor." Dexter laughs at the memory. "But I was still short. So the girl I was dating at the time--"

"Ah, there's always a girl, isn't there?"

Dexter swallows his salmon and washes it down with champagne. "I can tell you from experience that, yes, in most cases, there's always a girl at the heart of every good story."

Ruby laces her hands together and props her chin on them, listening with curiosity. "Okay, so you're sixteen, you have the car of your dreams, and you're madly in love."

"Oh, madly," Dexter says, smiling as he shakes his head. "I think at that point I'd proposed marriage, burned her any number of mixed CDs full of Radiohead and Linkin Park songs, and imagined us with three kids and a dog."

"Sounds about right for sixteen. I had a boyfriend at that age who I was sure I'd still be with at fifty, and yet here I am..."

"There was someone before Jack?" Dexter frowns. "I thought all First Ladies had to be pure and virginal."

"I think you're mixing up First Ladies and future queens. The expectations are slightly lower for First Ladies--but only slightly."

"I would imagine. I'm sure your past was deconstructed with a fine-tooth comb before you and Jack could proceed with even a first date."

Ruby laughs and her fork clinks against her plate. "Actually, I was working at an art gallery opening the night of our first date. A friend I knew hired young actors to pass around hors d'oeuvres and drinks, and Jack basically took the tray out of my hand and passed it off to another server. He wanted to leave right then and there and take me with him."

"So you went?" Dexter is watching her through his horn-rimmed glasses, his eyes burning with intensity.

"I hate to sound like the kind of woman who would abandon her post at a job in favor of a man, but...yeah, I did." Ruby sighs and her shoulders slump. She's thought of this night often, but not recently. Jack had been full of charm and sex appeal--what she's heard her daughters call "rizz" of late--and Ruby had been powerless to resist him. She'd barely put up a fight. She shakes her head now though, realizing what Dexter has done. "Hey! This is supposed to be about *you*. Let's get back to the magical sixteen-year-old girlfriend."

Dexter chuckles and surrenders. "Okay, I've been caught. I'll tell you more, since this lunch topic was supposed to be your choice. I was just letting the conversation go wherever it took us." He clears his throat. "Okay," he says, leaning forward in his chair like he's about to tell a huge tale. "I should first clarify that I was the one who was sixteen, and Amanda was actually nineteen." Ruby lifts both eyebrows but says nothing. "She and my older sister met at college and she'd come home with Nisha for the summer so they could work at the Jersey Shore together and save up for their own apartment that fall. They got jobs on the boardwalk and I tried to tag along as much as humanly possible, because as you can imagine, having a hot college girl living in my sister's bedroom all summer was a temptation that any sixteen-year-old boy would be hard-pressed to ignore."

"I am on the edge of my seat." Ruby holds her champagne flute in one hand as she listens with amusement.

"So Amanda...what can I say about Amanda. She was on the volley-ball team at Rutgers with my sister."

"This just keeps getting better and better."

"It does, so pay attention." Dexter has relaxed into his story and looks like he's having as much fun telling it as Ruby is hearing it. "I'll skip to the obvious part, which is that one afternoon while my sister was working a shift and Amanda was off, she came into my room and--yep, you guessed it--took my virginity, which I was only too happy to give. Truly. It was like a million teenage boy dreams had come to fruition, and I floated on a cloud for the next forty-eight hours, convinced that we were on the road to a happy life together."

"But..."

"Oh, you sensed that *but* in there?" Dexter glances around as the couple next to them signs their check and gets up to leave. "There is most definitely a *but* in there." The restaurant's speakers are playing a jazzy number that filters out onto the sidewalk. "So, I was ready to sell that Ford Fairlane and buy Amanda a promise ring."

"You were not."

"I was. You have no idea how hard a boy can fall for his first love. Anyhow, I'd picked out a very cute little heart-shaped emerald on a gold band that was going to cost me more than I'd earned all summer, *plus* the eight hundred dollars I'd nearly saved up for the paint job, when I went down to the boardwalk to surprise Amanda and, you know, maybe take her for a walk along the water on her break from work and tell her that I loved her."

Ruby's face contorts in sympathetic pain. "Oh, Dexter."

"Yeah..." He nods and lets his head hang for a second as he remembers it. "You know how this story is going to end. So I showed up right before her break was ending--bad luck on my part--and I was standing there at the milkshake shack waiting for her to get back when I spotted her holding hands with some guy."

"Noooooo!" Ruby's hands fly to her cheeks; she's completely invested in the heartbreak of what she imagines is a floppy-haired, smooth-cheeked, gangly version of grown-up Dexter. "She didn't!"

"She did. And I can't really blame her. This guy was totally built. He must have been twenty-eight and with arms the size of my thighs." Dexter puts both hands up and mimics trying to encircle this guy's massive leg. "He had a tattoo on one bicep that was like a full version of the *Mona Lisa*."

"Wait, he had the *Mona Lisa* on his arm? That's not what I was picturing."

"Yeah, it was an interesting choice, but my point is, that man's arm was a full-sized canvas. At sixteen, you could have maybe fit one of her eyes on my tiny bicep before having to wrap her face around and into my armpit."

Ruby tries not to laugh at this image because she doesn't want to insult Dexter, but she glances into his eyes and sees that he's completely aware of the hilarity of himself as a scrawny, lovelorn sixteen-year-old boy stumbling onto the woman of his dreams holding hands with a fully-grown man. She smothers the urge to laugh until Dexter breaks into a huge grin.

"I'm cool with it. You can laugh," he says, running a hand through his sandy hair. Ruby watches his every move, admiring how self-assured and funny he is. As she's gotten to know Dexter over the past couple of

<figure>66</figure>

months, she's been increasingly aware of the way he approaches the world. With everything, whether it's her stories about her marriage, or his outlook on life, Dexter is someone who takes everything in with deep intensity. He listens--really listens--to Ruby, to the news, to the waiter telling them the daily specials, to his thoughts inside his own head (she's definitely observed him doing this).

"Well, I'm not laughing *at* you," Ruby clarifies, still hiding her smile behind one hand. "But I do have to ask how this ended up being the best year of your life when, to be honest, it sounds pretty tragic."

"Oh, well that's the good part." Dexter is hunched over his plate, staying close enough to Ruby that they can have this conversation in lowered voices. "Not only did I see Amanda holding hands with this giant Arnold Schwarzenegger imposter, but as he dropped her back off at the milkshake shack, he leaned in and kissed her—like a full-on, tongue down the throat, eyes closed kind of kiss—and he actually picked her up off the ground by holding both of her butt cheeks in his hands." He mimes a cupping motion with his hands and Ruby's mouth drops open.

"I'm still not seeing the silver lining of this dark cloud," she says, shaking her head so that her hair brushes over her shoulders.

Dexter sits back in his chair. "The silver lining is that after picking up the pieces of my absolutely shattered young heart, I realized that I'd already gone through my first traumatic romantic experience. I was determined that it would only go uphill from there. And I also under-stood that sometimes things are out of your hands and that you just have to accept them as they come."

"That's a lot for a sixteen-year-old." Ruby pushes her plate aside and reaches for her ice water. "But I have to ask, were you able to carry on with that same determination? Did your love life only go uphill from there?"

Dexter snorts. "Of course not! I'm a straight man who loves with his whole heart. Some of the finest people in your tribe—"

"My tribe? As in other women?"

"Precisely. Some of those women have given me a run for my money, but I wouldn't have it any other way."

"Why is that—that you wouldn't have it any other way?"

"Because," Dexter says, as if this is the most obvious thing in the world, "then my life would have taken a different path and I wouldn't be sitting here with you."

Ruby flushes, but it's true; she's well aware that any slight deviation from your path in life takes you on an entirely different journey. "That's a solid enough reason for me."

Dexter pays the bill and they stand, leaving their napkins on the table next to their empty glasses and the leather folder with the signed copy of the credit card slip tucked inside.

"Shall we?" Dexter holds out a hand to indicate that Ruby should lead the way.

They walk out onto Broadway and join the fray of humanity as it worms its way through the city streets. There's a pleasant afternoon breeze, but the sky is so clear and so pristine that Ruby feels like she can look straight up and see forever.

"What would you say to heading to Fort Tryon Park?" Dexter asks, walking with his hands in the pockets of his olive green canvas jacket. He's wearing a cream colored cable knit sweater under that, with a pair of worn-in blue jeans and brown boots, and Ruby is struck again by how incredibly attractive he is—so much so that she forgets to notice that people turn their heads and point at her as she walks by.

"Sure, I'd love to," she says, feeling like a giddy girl who just got asked to go for a stroll by the captain of the football team. It's a strange reversal of reality, as Ruby is by far the most looked at and well-known of the two of them, but when she's walking with Dexter, she absolutely feels as if *he's* the somebody and that *she's* just a smitten girl following him around with a goofy grin on her face.

They hop into a taxi with Banks sitting silently in the front seat next to the driver while Ruby and Dexter sit in the back, and end up at the park in under ten minutes. The driver casts sideways glances at Banks the entire time, looking as though he wants to ask questions, but he doesn't.

Ruby stands on the sidewalk while Dexter pays the driver and then slides out of the backseat and closes the door.

"Ready?" he says, offering her an arm, which she takes. Banks follows them at a slight distance.

It turns out that Fort Tryon Park is home to the Linden Terrace, one of the highest points in Manhattan, and from that particular spot, you can see across the water to the Hudson River Palisades, with its miles and miles of fiery orange and gold foliage blanketing the surrounding cliffs.

Ruby and Dexter wander over the stone paths, passing under old and mossy brick arches with walkways overhead as they talk about their lives, their parents, and the things they like and don't like. (Ruby: loves sweaters, fireplaces, the smell of the ocean, margaritas with extra salt, and her children; hates: having the flu, when tragic things happen to people, ratatouille, and the creepy ticking of the clock on *60 Minutes*. Dexter: loves the color orange, watching spy movies, spicy foods, and Iceland; hates: car exhaust in traffic, being stuck on the tarmac inside an airplane, nightmares, and running into people he knew in high school.) As far as Ruby is concerned, it's all feeling comfortable and cozy and—dare she even think it?—*date-like* until they find a bench on the banks that overlook the water. They sit next to one another facing the wash of fall colors in the trees on the other side of the Hudson River and are quiet for a moment, basking in the particular feel of the autumn afternoon sun.

"I'd like to ask you about whether you think Jack ever had an affair before Etienne," Dexter says, breaking the spell of hazy warmth that Ruby has allowed to wrap around her like a blanket.

"Oh," she says, feeling her stomach plummet like a roller coaster that's just crested the peak and gone into free-fall. "Right."

Dexter shifts next to her on the bench and turns his upper body so that he's looking right at Ruby, but she refuses to look his way. "I'm sorry—I didn't mean to drop that right into the middle of what was otherwise a fun and lighthearted conversation. That was my fault."

"No, no," Ruby says, catching herself before she agrees. "We're here to talk about the hard stuff, and I know that. But you can't blame a girl for wanting to stick to easier topics."

"Right. And it's all helpful for me to know," Dexter says. "You know—for the book."

Right. For the book. Ruby swallows hard. "Okay, shifting gears."

Dexter stays still, but even from two feet away, Ruby can feel the change in the energy between them; he's aware that he's altered the chemistry of the afternoon, and that the only way to fix things is to be quiet and see what Ruby says next.

"Actually, I don't know whether he did or didn't," she says after giving it some thought. "And I'm not sure that it even matters. The fact that Jack carried on a full-fledged relationship with another woman and fathered a child with her so completely supersedes anything else that he might have done that it's...kind of a moot point. At least to me."

Dexter nods, listening. "Do you feel like you can ever forgive him for his transgressions?"

"I don't know. I'd like to, if only for the fact that I think it's unhealthy to live the rest of my life holding on to any type of anger. That can't be good, can it?"

"Probably not. But people have different capacities for forgiveness, and you have to decide for yourself what you can live with and what you can't."

"Of course." Ruby watches a crew row past on the river, their upper bodies covered with long-sleeved white jerseys, but their strong legs visible from under matching red shorts. "I think the hardest part was feeling that I might not have known who Jack truly was at all. It was the first time I ever felt like I might be married to a stranger. That he was part of a machine that I had no understanding of. Here I'd been thinking all along that I was married to a man who believed in his stances and his politics, but who came home at night to his wife and daughters and switched off the Jack Hudson Persona to just become Jack, or Dad. I was wrong though. So, so wrong." Her voice gets quieter. "He was someone else entirely."

Dexter lets that sit there for a long moment and then taps his fingers gently on the bench behind Ruby's back, as his arm is still resting there. "I'm not just blowing hot air up your skirt because I've grown to really like and respect you, but I think it's fair to say that one of you was putting your true, authentic self into this marriage, and it wasn't Jack."

Ruby is pulled from her reverie; she turns her head to look at Dexter. "Are you allowed to interject that way?"

Dexter blinks in surprise. "You mean, am I allowed as the interviewer to put in my two cents? To have a personal opinion?"

70

"Yeah, I guess." Ruby squints at him like she's forgotten that someone is even listening to her recollections. "I mean, does that taint the material in any way?"

"Well..." Dexter turns his body to face the water, pulling his arm off the bench behind Ruby. "Journalists have their own code of ethics and two of the important rules are to be objective and impartial."

"And are you?" It's Ruby's turn to stare at the side of his face as she waits for an answer.

Dexter stays quiet for a long moment. "I will be when I write the book," he says carefully. "But am I actually impartial?" He finally turns his head to look at her again. "Let me be as honest as I can with you: no."

Ruby holds his gaze. "I'm not impartial about you, either."

Without another word, they both look out across the Hudson and let their eyes settle on the foliage and the natural beauty that this gorgeous day has to offer, disappearing into their own thoughts.

After hours and hours of productive late-night Zoom calls, forty-eight hours together on Christmas Key over the summer talking about serious topics, and just four hours together in New York City today, Ruby and Dexter have come to an impasse: neither one of them is completely objective about the other, and while the conversation isn't going to go any further than it already has, they've inadvertently turned a corner in their working relationship, and neither one of them knows how to go back.

So instead, they just look at the leaves.

Sunday

It's just as arduous a journey to Tangier Island as Sunday remembers, and she takes it this time with a sense of foreboding, fearful of what could possibly happen.

With her on the ferry for the hour-long ride from the banks of Onancock are her daughters—one happily along for the ride, and the other sullen and withdrawn. The ferry stops running for winter by mid-October, which adds a sense of urgency to the trip for Sunday: it's now or never. She either goes to Tangier and shows her daughters her tangled roots, or she waits for spring, giving Peter ample time to drag her life out for the entertainment of the public at large.

"This is gorgeous," Olive says, her long, dark hair blowing out like a silky fan behind her as the ferry traverses the water.

And it is lovely to look at: the water isn't quite a dark, Atlantic Ocean navy blue here, but a prettier Yale blue that almost feels exotic. In the distance, Tangier looms like a giant floating marsh, so flat that Sunday remembers the feeling of walking around on the ground and wondering if Tangier might someday squish like a wet sponge beneath the feet of all who tread on its sandy shores. It's always felt to her like the island itself is sinking, being swallowed up by salty water, drowning in its own fluids while people stand on the mainland watching, thankful that they aren't living on an island lost in time and waterlogged by the sea. Its tiny island feel is entirely different and a world apart from the warm, tropical vibe of Shipwreck Key, and Sunday gives a shiver of gratitude for her new home as the ferry approaches the dock.

She hasn't told anyone that she's coming, and she prefers it that way. The only chance she has of showing her daughters Tangier Island and of giving them a view of her early life is if she does it entirely on her own terms, with no obligations to visit anyone else. As the ferry pulls in and people start to shuffle off the boat, Sunday turns around to look for Cameron, who chose to ride inside rather than out on the bow of the ferry with her and Olive. Sure enough, Cameron is coming through a rusted door, her camel colored wool trench coat wrapped around her tiny waist, and a pair of dark sunglasses covering her eyes.

"You ready, babe?" Sunday asks her, motioning for Cameron to follow her.

Cameron sighs audibly.

"Welcome to Tangier Island," a man in a pair of paint-splattered overalls greets the ferry passengers with a tip of his head. His eyes land on Sunday and linger there for just a moment longer than she likes. "Well, well, well. The prodigal daughter returns." For Sunday, he gives not just a tip of his head, but he lifts the sweat-stained green cap off the top of his nearly bald head and bows his chin reverently. "Welcome home, Mrs. Bond."

Sunday cringes at the word "home"; it's been years since she thought of home as anything but the place she lives with Peter or her daughters. She's gotten used to thinking of Shipwreck Key as home just about as quickly as she shed the skin of a Tangier Islander on the ferry the last time she left this place, so to see it now through the eyes of a woman who is entirely different than the girl who'd left this place is unsettling.

"Mom!" Olive says, tugging at her right arm. "I can't believe this is your home. I always felt like you just grew up in Washington."

They walk down the long, weathered dock together, with Cameron following behind them, holding the handles of her artfully worn-in Louis Vuitton duffel bag in one manicured hand.

"I basically *did* grow up in Washington," Sunday says, letting Olive slip her hand through her arm so that they can walk with their shoulders pressed together. "But this is technically where I'm from. I hope it's not too much of a letdown for you girls." She drops her voice. "It's a fairly modest place, and the people here are hardworking and not into frills or fame."

"But that guy knew you," Olive says, turning her head to look back at the older man in the overalls.

"Everyone knows Mom," Cameron says, slipping her sunglasses off and shooting Olive a steely glare. "Plus she lived here until she was sixteen, so it's not like there aren't going to be a ton of people here who know her."

Sunday pauses before stopping at the end of the dock and addressing Cameron. "That's true," she says. "There are people who know me as the girl I was, and we will definitely run into some of them. I don't know what they'll say," she says, looking back and forth between her daughters, "and I can't control what impression you get of me from these interactions, but I want you to know that I brought you here so that you could learn more about the real me."

"We know the real you, Mom," Cameron says, looking bored. "The real you is all about spin control. Daddy is going to run for office again, and you know that it's going to look bad for you to be living your bachelorette life down in Florida while he's busting his butt on the campaign trail, so you want to come here and show the world that you're still the same down-home girl from a small town. But you're not. You're a calculating woman who probably left this dump behind without a second thought." Cameron flings the hand that's not holding her duffel bag in the direction of the activity on the main street of the island. "You went to D.C. to find a man, and you found one. Then you stayed with him even though he treated you like crap for years."

"Hold on a second," Sunday says, putting a hand up to stop her daughter. There are people from the ferry streaming around them, though they can't help but hear a little of the conversation that Sunday and her girls are having right there on the dock. "If you think I stayed with him for too long and that he treated me so badly, then why are you always on his side, Cam?"

Cameron rolls her eyes and looks put out for a moment, then turns to look at her mother directly. "I'm on his side because Daddy never pretended to be anything he wasn't. He might be a gay man trapped in a straight man's world—"

Olive makes a huffing sound like she can't believe her sister just said this out loud. "Cam, come on," she says, looking around to make sure that no one has heard this.

"But at least Dad is clear about who he is—he's a politician," Cameron goes on. "You pretended to be this perfect wife who stood by her husband's side, but you only did it so that you could escape from whatever this place is." Cameron stops her tirade for a second and casts her gaze at the buildings that are visible from where they are. It's mostly white-painted wooden houses, businesses, and bicycles with rusty fenders from exposure to the salty sea air. Every so often a golf cart slips by, driven by someone who is waving or shouting out friendly greetings to people on the sidewalks.

"You have no idea," Sunday whispers with sadness. "I had to leave here, whether I wanted to or not."

"Cam," Olive interrupts her mother and sister, "if you're going to act this way, then why did you even come? I thought you might at least show up and listen to what Mom has to say."

Olive's words seem to soften Cameron just a bit, and the tightness of her posture loosens perceptibly. "I do want to hear what she has to say. It's important to me."

Sunday's eyes immediately sting with unshed tears; her baby girl is here, and she's willing to listen and find out what Sunday had gone through as a young girl. She's about to thank Cameron for being there when Cameron speaks instead.

"I need to know everything that made you the way you are, Mom. I want to find out all the things you did and why you did them, and then I want to make sure I don't repeat your mistakes with my own kids."

The tears in Sunday's eyes well insistently and she can feel herself on the verge of a sob; this was not what she'd hoped to hear from Cameron.

Cameron holds her Louis Vuitton like she's about to turn around and stalk back onto the ferry, leaving Olive and Sunday behind on the island. And she probably would, which Sunday knows from raising this headstrong, tough-as-nails woman, but the ferry has already pulled away to head back to the booming metropolis of Onancock, so she stays put there on the dock, holding her mother's gaze in hers.

"I need to figure out how to get it right," Cameron says, laying a hand protectively across her midsection. "Because I just found out that I'm pregnant."

* * *

Sunday stumbles around the little house that she's rented on Airbnb. She'd been shocked to find that the world of vacation rentals had actually reached Tangier Island, but when she'd plugged in the data and searched, sure enough, there was a tiny three-bedroom house overlooking the water for rent. It had been advertised as a "charming beach bungalow" with "amenities galore," but Sunday knows Tangier well enough that she wasn't fooled for a second: the house is a single-story, clapboard dwelling with a mudroom off the front porch. This repository for mucky boots, jackets, and hats has huge windows that look out onto the marshy water, and the sunsets from the mudroom are undoubtedly the kind that bathe a person in the golden light of evening, making them feel warmed from the outside in as they shed outerwear and step into the folds of the house.

But the house itself is rustic, at best. A handmade table and chairs sit next to a wood stove in the kitchen (this had been offered up in the ad as a "breakfast nook," but is the only dining option for every meal), and the bedrooms are all small and clean, each with a four-poster bed covered in a simple white duvet. Everyone shares a single bathroom with a pedestal sink and a narrow shower, and the linen closet is filled with soft, well-worn towels and bedsheets. It is precisely what Sunday expected, but seeing her daughters here is jarring; their whole lives have been spent ferrying from upscale hotels in major cities to resort destinations, and while Olive seems overly charmed by the paintings of the sea framed and hung on the walls in every room, Cameron looks slightly out of place there, twisting the pearl necklace she wears over a black cashmere turtleneck as she observes the plain surroundings.

"Is this what your house looked like, Mom?" Olive asks, standing next to Sunday at the kitchen counter while she makes tea for the three of them. "This place has got such a rustic, simple vibe. I love it."

"Thanks, babe," Sunday says. She knows her younger daughter is working overtime to stay cheerful and upbeat, and she appreciates Olive's efforts to mitigate the storm that's brewing between her and Cameron. "And yes, my house was much like this one. My dad and brother used to come in off the water after a long day of fishing and dump all their wet and dirty clothes in the front room." She places teabags in three heavy ceramic mugs and pours the boiling water from the kettle over each, watching as the steam curls up and away.

"You don't talk much about any of that," Olive says, taking two mugs by the handles and walking them to the table. She sets one carefully in front of Cameron and then sits down in a chair with her own tea. Sunday brings the last mug over and sits with her daughters beneath the simple chandelier that hangs over the table. The sun is already low in the sky, and there's a slight chill in the air that makes her want to put some logs in the wood stove and start a nice fire.

"I've told you both that my brother died young, and you've met your aunt Minnie--my sister--do either of you remember that?"

Olive and Cameron give each other a long look and Cameron lifts a shoulder and lets it fall. "Not really." She looks less guarded in this moment, and curious about the story her mother is telling.

"She came to Washington when you girls were fairly young and brought her kids, Matt and A.J. I think we took you all to the Lincoln Memorial and to a street fair. You kids all got your faces painted like animals--Cam, you were a tiger, and Ollie, you chose a zebra--and then one of you ate too many hot dogs and got a stomach ache, though I can't remember which one of you it was." Sunday lifts her mug of tea with both hands and blows on the steam to cool it. "That was the only time Minnie came to visit, and I never brought you two here."

Cameron's face hardens again. "And why didn't you ever bring us back here to Tangier? I mean, look around--this would have been a great place for two little girls to play with their cousins. We landed at the boat dock and right away we saw a shop that sells candy, plus there were kids running around with fishing poles. I would imagine there were even more children here when we were young."

Sunday nods, but doesn't refute this. "That's all true. It would have been a place where you could have come each summer and made memories with family, but I chose not to bring you."

"See, this is exactly what I'm talking about," Cameron says, pounding a fist on the wooden table and making everyone's tea slosh around in their mugs. "When I'm a mother, I want to make sure my kids know where I come from."

"So you're going to just take them on a White House tour?" Olive asks with a touch of sarcasm. "Take them for lunch at the National Cathedral School?" she says, mentioning the private girls' school that they both attended, along with the daughters of nearly every politician in Washington. Olive shoots her sister a look. "Come on, Cam. There will be things you leave out with your kids. Mom probably has her reasons."

"I do," Sunday says, picking up her cue. "And they're damn good ones." With this, she stands up and walks over to the small window above the kitchen sink. It has the same view as the windows from the mud room, though now that the sun has sunk halfway into Chesapeake Bay, the autumn half-light has changed from a warm gold to a thin, watery yellow.

"I want to hear everything," Olive says, watching her mother from the chair at the table. "I'm here with an open heart, Mom."

Cameron sighs audibly. "Always the overachiever," she says, shaking her head with pity. "It's obvious that you've got a complex, Ol."

Olive turns to her sister with a hard frown. "A complex about what?"

"Being adopted, probably."

"Oh, that's rich. Like you aren't adopted."

"Yeah, but I'm fine with it. You're always trying to prove something."

"Like what?" Olive asks, looking and sounding as offended as she should look and sound in the face of this kind of accusation.

"I have no idea, because I've accepted my reality." Cameron looks out the window with a haughty expression. "I have no idea who my parents are, and the people who adopted me are semi-strangers."

"Cameron!" Sunday sucks in a sharp breath. She instantly starts to cry, turning her back to the girls as she faces the sink and the window. She hadn't meant to burst into tears.

Olive stands up sharply, pushing her chair back as she walks over to their mother. "Hey, Mom," she says, putting her arms around Sunday and resting her chin on her mother's shoulder as she hugs her from behind. "Cam's just working through stuff. Ignore her."

Sunday shakes her head, her chin falling to her chest. "I can't ignore her, babe. She speaks the truth, even if it isn't a truth I like hearing."

They stay like this, together in the kitchen but in their separate spaces, silently letting their reality sink in. Cameron rests her chin on her hand, elbow on the table, watching her mom and sister; Olive holds her mother, not wanting to let her go; Sunday keeps her back to her girls, aware that they truly *don't* know her yet, but fearing that when they do, they may not respect or love her at all.

She pulls herself together, wiping at her eyes and nose before she breaks free of Olive's grasp and turns to face them both. "Get your coats, girls. We're going out. It's time for you to meet your mother."

Ruby

Dexter is waiting in the lobby of Ruby's hotel again that evening, cooling his heels at the bar as she slips on one pair of ballet flats, deems them all wrong, and tosses them on the floor behind her. In a hurry, she slips on her ankle boots again and yanks off a soft pink sweater, exchanging it for a tight black one that hugs her body and ends at the waistband of her tight jeans. Ruby stands before the full-length mirror in the bathroom, turning from side to side; she actually looks good. This will work. Her strict schedule of running and working out have fallen by the wayside during her time on Shipwreck Key, and while her toned physique has softened a bit, the sun has kissed her shoulders, nose, and forehead, leaving her with a golden glow and strands of bright blonde woven through her hair.

She's about to text Dexter and let him know that she's coming when her phone chimes with an incoming email. Ruby tosses a red lipstick into her crossbody bag and slips on a cropped leather jacket, then flicks the message open, skimming it. It's from Etienne Boucher. She drops her purse on the floor and the lipstick rolls out. Ruby sits heavily on the foot of the bed, holding her phone in her hand.

Ruby--

I waited a few months before reaching out to you because I wanted to give you some space, but we need to talk. It will be uncomfortable, and yet, it is necessary. Jack has always taken care of Julien financially, and he had set up a life insurance policy with Julien as the main beneficiary, however I am now unable to collect on it.

When Jack died, the world believed it was an accident, and an accident would be fully covered under this policy. I had very nearly finished the paperwork to collect the funds when you revealed to the world that he had, in fact, taken his own life. Because of this, the policy was denied. I now have no recourse and no help in raising Julien.

As Jack's legal wife, your life and your future are not in question. Ours is. Can we talk?

Etienne

Ruby's hand goes slack and her phone falls against her thigh. This was not a message she ever wanted to receive, and reading it here, in New York where she's already up to her eyebrows in the minutia of her marriage and of Jack's duplicitous life choices, feels like yet another pound of heavy weight that she'll have to carry.

With a sigh, she stands up, bends to pick up her purse and the lipstick, and shoves everything into the bag, zipping it. She calls Banks from her room phone to tell him that she's ready to head out, then turns out the light and heads to the lobby.

* * *

Dexter, who had parted ways with Ruby on Broadway after their trip to Fort Tryon Park that afternoon, is waiting for her at the bar. His elbows are resting on the sleek wood in front of him, and he's nursing a bourbon on the rocks.

"Get you one?" he offers, holding up his highball glass.

Ruby sinks onto the stool next to his. "I shouldn't drink this evening. I'll just get sloppy and sentimental, and I want to stay focused for your questions. I need to give you what you're looking for, not a heaping mess of 'Ruby stuff' to untangle."

Jack downs the last sip of bourbon and sets the glass on the counter. "I'm a master at untangling stuff, but I hear you. I don't want you to say anything you don't want to tell me." He stands, opens his wallet, and leaves a twenty on the counter. "I've got plans for us this evening. Shall we?"

Ruby follows him out of the bar, through the hotel lobby, and out onto the street, where the sun has just set. As they walk, Dexter explains that he's taking her to a Halloween flotilla parade.

Ruby's spirit lightens just a smidge and she turns to him, holding the strap of her purse across her body. "Oh! I've heard of that--it's gorgeous at night with the pumpkins all lit up. But we don't have one to send out on the water."

Dexter smiles at her, looking amused. "I think it's okay if we just observe. Unless you want to track down a pumpkin, carve it in a hurry, find a candle for it, and enter it in the flotilla parade."

Ruby grabs onto his arm with a laugh; Dexter is onto her, because that *was* her first thought, unreasonable though it is.

"Okay," she says. "Let's just go watch then."

"I thought it would be fun. Maybe we can sit on the grass and just take it all in while we chat."

They walk quietly for a couple of minutes, dodging other pedestrians and crossing the streets at traffic lights. At one point, Dexter reaches for her hand and holds it as they race around the bumper of a car and cut in front of a honking taxi with its headlights slicing through the twilight. Ruby forgets entirely that Banks is shadowing them, but when she remembers and throws a glance over her shoulder, he's right there, watching her and everyone around her like a hawk.

"This city is an obstacle course," Ruby says breathlessly, following Dexter down into the subway. "We're not taking a taxi?"

"Let's travel like locals," Dexter says, swiping his Metro card three times so that they can both pass through the turnstiles and Banks can pass through after them.

"You *are* a local," Ruby says, standing next to him on the platform and feeling the energy of the trains on their tracks in the distance as it courses into the soles of her feet and vibrates through her body.

"Stick with me kid—we'll go places," Dexter says in a deep growl, imitating a forties-style gangster movie. This makes Ruby laugh again, and she realizes that she laughs more with Dexter than she does in the presence of nearly anybody else.

"Alright," Ruby says, looking at him with a smile as he waits for the next train. "I'll stick with you."

When they exit the subway station at 86th Street they're at the edge of Central Park, and even though it's still the first week of October, there are kids everywhere dressed in costumes, with parents close behind carrying carved pumpkins. There are also adults in varying degrees of fancy dress: wigs, makeup, crazy clothes, and there's even a man walking on stilts and wearing a gigantic cowboy hat.

"I feel underdressed," Ruby says, glancing down at her black leather jacket-sweater-jeans-ankle boots look. "I mean, I'm in head-to-toe black, which can either be seen as standard New York attire, or I guess it could work for Halloween."

"You look chic," Dexter decides, looking her up and down. He's wearing another variation of his jeans, army green overcoat, and boots look, but tonight he's also got a blue Yankees cap pulled down over his dark blonde hair. "Let's find a spot by the water." Again, he takes her by the hand, pulling her through the crowd of people as everyone makes their way to a spot where they can either watch or participate in the flotilla parade.

Ruby turns to Banks, who is standing closer to her than usual, given the sizable crowd. "Is this fine?" she asks him quietly. Normally he prefers to know where they're going in advance, but she and Dexter have been operating differently, and therefore she never knows where she might end up.

"This is fine, ma'am," he reassures her, clenching and unclenching his jaw as his eyes graze the crowd around them. He's so close that Ruby can smell his aftershave, while normally he stays back several paces.

Dexter and Ruby find a patch of grass to sit on, and Banks picks a spot beneath a tree where he can survey the area. They settle in to observe as people take their pumpkins down to the water's edge. There, the organizers of the event are helping people get their candles lit and their pumpkins set on squares of foam that will float under the weight of the jack-o'-lanterns. Within minutes, the water is filled with little rafts of floating lights, the jagged smiles and elaborate faces of the pumpkins emitting a golden glow that sparkles and dances off the water against the evening sky.

"This is lovely," Ruby says, sitting close enough to Dexter that she can hear him breathe. The night air is autumnal, but not yet cold. "Having something to watch while we talk is making this easier."

"Good. I'm glad." Dexter has his legs stretched out in front of him and he's leaning back on his hands for support as he turns to look at Ruby. "I know some of these topics are ones you've been bracing yourself for, but I also know the book is going to be better for our ability to have an open conversation."

Ruby nods and folds her legs into a criss-cross style. Her stretchy black jeans were the perfect choice for the evening, and she sits with her elbows on her knees, hands dangling towards the ground so that she can pluck little blades of grass as she listens.

"You know a lot about me already," Ruby says, not looking at Dexter. "More than most people. We've covered so many things in our nightly talks, and you were there when I first read the letter from Jack. I trust you, Dex," she says, calling him a nickname that she doesn't normally use, trying it on for size so that she can gauge his reaction.

"I want you to know that you can trust me, and that I do value your feelings and your comfort with our discussions, as well as the integrity of this book—my earlier transgression aside."

"No, no," Ruby says, looking up at him as she drops the blades of grass in her hands. She'd had a few hours to herself after their time at Fort Tryon Park, and the memory of Dexter interjecting his personal opinion had played over and over in her mind. "It didn't bother me that you did, I just wasn't sure...how that might play out in your writing if you started to feel strongly one way or the other about things like my marriage."

The unspoken words hang between them for a moment, and Ruby imagines that they're both thinking them: *And that our co-admissions of impartiality won't impact our work together.*

"I understand." Dexter nods and presses his lips together as he watches a little girl of about eight or nine set her pumpkin on a flotilla and push it out into the water. It's been carved to look like a fish bowl with bubbles and fish swimming all along the pumpkin's skin. The girl is dressed like a mermaid. "I'll try not to do it again, if you think it in any way jeopardizes our work together, but Ruby..."

"I don't think that it does," Ruby says quickly, filling the silence that she anticipated might be filled with something else. "I trust your judgment, your professionalism, and where this book is going. I truly do. You are an amazing writer, Dex," she says, "and I want us to put out the best damn book possible. I mean you—I want *you* to put out the best book. Sorry, I wasn't trying to make it ours or anything. You know what I mean." Ruby blushes like a nervous teenage girl.

"It's ours, Ruby," he says, staring at her with a long look that's full of meaning and unspoken words. "When you work this closely with someone on a project that's this intimate, you don't get to take full credit for it as an author. Is my name on it? Sure, but the world will know that this is *our* book. We'll do a press tour—if I can convince you to join me—and it will give you a platform to say whatever it is you might want to say."

Ruby laughs. "You think I'll still have more to share after we go over every single day of my life from birth to age fifty?"

"Probably. Because the minute the book is published, your life goes on. The days stack up, and you have more feelings, more life experiences, more opinions to share. This book won't be a capsule of your entire life from start to finish, it will just be the highlights of the first half century."

Ruby sputters at the term *half century*. "God, that makes me sound ancient."

"You're not," Dexter says quickly. "Not even close."

They sit in silence and watch more children and adults bring their pumpkins to the edge of the water and send them out to float under the October moon. Central Park at night is lit from the windows of the buildings that surround it, but also by the rows of tall lantern lights on lampposts along the paths. There's a relaxed feeling to the evening, and the people around Ruby and Dexter are chatting amiably and sharing bottles of wine, food from coolers, and photographing or taking video of everything around them. Ruby feels like she's been invited to a neighborhood block party.

"Can we talk about the day Jack died?" Ruby ventures, wanting to dive in. She's not going to make the same mistake she made earlier in the afternoon at Fort Tryon Park, getting so comfortable that she forgets the real reason that she's here with Dexter; this isn't a date, and she needs to remember that whenever she starts to feel like they're just chatting for the purpose of getting to know one another better.

Dexter nods, clearly trying to look casual about broaching one of the bigger topics that they need to cover. "Sure. Of course we can." He takes out his phone, opens the voice memo app, and holds it up wordlessly for her approval before he starts recording.

Ruby nods and blows out a breath. She brings herself back to that day, the feelings of which are a sharp contrast to how she's feeling right now, in this particular moment. She tries to recall the shock, the horror, the stabbing physical pain of knowing that Jack was really and truly gone—forever.

"I was in a meeting in the dining room at the White House, and Jack's Chief of Staff—"

"Helen Pullman."

"Exactly. Helen, who is an extremely close friend of mine—she, Sunday, and I are actually a very tight trio—came and told me she needed to talk. I followed her to the sitting room in our private residence, and she dove right in and told me the news. She said we didn't have a lot of time to waste, as there were just minutes to spare before the entire world would find out, and that she'd already arranged for my girls to be brought back to the White House by private car so that they weren't in airports or surrounded by anyone who might break the news to them first. She'd thought of everything, and it was truly a kindness to have someone at the helm who was so well prepared."

"Disconcerting though, right? To have a person so close to you but so well-versed in the protocol surrounding your husband's untimely death?"

"Yes, of course. It was bizarre. Otherworldly. We'd all been prepped for a worst case scenario event. It's almost like practicing hurricane drills or something at school, but then having an actual hurricane blow onto your campus and tear the roof off the building without warning. You sit there for a minute like, 'What do I do? Duck? Hide? Run for cover?' But Helen took me by the hand and walked me straight through it. I wouldn't have survived those early days without her."

"I know what your reaction was when you read his letter for the first time because I sat across from you and watched your face, but what were you told in those first minutes, and how did you respond?"

Ruby closes her eyes and remembers. "I was told that he was not in the U.K. as I'd been led to believe, but instead had crashed into the Bay of Biscay off the coast of France. I was really hung up on the fact that he was in a different country than I'd originally thought. I'm not sure why, but that got stuck in my brain and I almost couldn't push that aside to process that he was dead. My next thought was that Jack was an excellent pilot. He'd had a pilot's license for about forty-five years, and had been a pilot in the Air Force. And then beyond that, I wondered how in the hell the sitting President of the United States ends up flying a single engine plane instead of being ferried on Air Force One. My mind was doing loops and circles just trying to digest and process it all. Truly."

"I can't even begin to imagine. At what point did you put two and two together in terms of him being in France?"

"Well, it hadn't been that long since our breakfast in Palm Beach where Harlow had confronted him with the results of her DNA test, and with the fact that a boy in France was a potential half-sibling for her. Which, as you recall, he denied without so much as batting an eye. We still hadn't had the chance to sit down and properly hash that one out, so while I wanted answers, I'd been waiting for the right time to talk to him. And that right time never came before the accident." Dexter gives her a long, searching look. "I guess it wasn't really an accident was it? What do you call it when something that's normally considered a tragic accident is actually done on purpose?"

"I would call it a decision that ends in tragedy."

"Mmm," Ruby says, nodding in agreement. "That's truly what it was."

They sit in peaceful silence, watching as hundreds of pumpkins bob on the water, glowing with light.

"Do you wish he'd made a different decision? Perhaps told you about his illness?"

Ruby considers this. The letter that Jack's mistress had delivered to her a year after his death—at his request—had enlightened her to the fact that he'd been diagnosed with a rare and incurable neurological disorder called Creutzfeldt-Jakob disease. The only outcome for someone diagnosed with Creutzfeldt-Jakob disease is death, and generally quite swiftly. Many people only live for six to eight months, and degeneration happens nearly overnight. Jack hadn't wanted to see that ending, and so he'd done what he thought he needed to do to spare himself, his family, and the entire country from watching him die a fast, unpleasant death.

"I'm not sure," Ruby says honestly.

A toddler in a pink fairy outfit complete with iridescent wings runs toward them with her arms open, but the little girl's mother swoops in and picks her up just before she reaches Ruby. The mother smiles at Ruby benignly, but then her eyes light up with recognition. Ruby gives her a nod of understanding, but then turns back to Dexter; she doesn't want to lose this train of thought, even to share pleasantries with a young mother who has just realized that her little girl was stumbling right into the arms of a former First Lady.

"Had Jack told me what was going on, I know I would have jumped into 'fix it' mode. That's just how I am. I would have consulted the best doctors and specialists in the world, and filled his last days and months with trials, treatments, and little events and things meant to build memories for all of us—particularly for Harlow and Athena. But that might not have been what Jack wanted. I mean, obviously it wasn't. It's possible that he would have wanted to end his days in the south of France with his..." Ruby pauses here, looking stricken. "With his other family. Maybe he would have wanted her to attend to his needs. Or possibly he would have preferred to have his son running in and out of the room, telling him about school, or about the games he was playing with his friends. How am I to ever know now which of his lives Jack preferred more?" Ruby feels herself growing hysterical at her own question, one to which she'll never have an answer.

"I suppose you won't ever know," Dexter agrees. He's pulled his knees up and has his arms wrapped loosely around them, back rounded as he leans in to listen to Ruby. "But would you really want to?"

Ruby has no idea: *would* she really want answers to every question that's gone through her mind as she's lain in bed all these nights since Jack's death? Probably not. Like many things in life, it's the *not* knowing that allows us to suspend our disbelief enough to go on.

"I guess not," she finally says. "And furthermore—much like the question of whether he'd been unfaithful before Etienne—it doesn't much matter now. It ended the way it ended, and I'm still in the same position I'd be in regardless." She stares at the ground in front of her. "Before I came down to the bar tonight, I got an email from Etienne." It's the first she's mentioned of it all evening, and she wasn't even sure she would tell Dexter about it until this very moment.

"Oh?" Dexter bristles next to her. "If you're up for sharing, I'd love to hear more about it."

"Of course." Ruby takes her phone from her purse, opens the email, and hands it over to Dexter so he can read it for himself.

His face is lit by the glow of her phone screen as his eyes skim the message from top to bottom, then his gaze flicks back to the top and he reads it again.

"Shit," Dexter says, finally handing the phone back. "This is incredibly bold of her."

"I thought so. I have no idea how to respond or even what to do, aside from consulting my attorney, obviously."

"A logical first step."

"I don't feel any obligation to help her support her child, if I'm being perfectly honest, and I think it's outrageous that she's come to me with this. The angry, hurt part of me is thinking, 'Well, what did you expect when you got involved with a married man? Sorry-not-sorry.' Which I think is a fair way for a woman to feel."

Dexter looks like he's holding back his personal opinion, as promised. Instead, he asks his next question: "What are your hopes for your daughters and their long-term contact with Jack's son?"

Ruby's eyebrows shoot up. "I have no idea what I truly want. No, actually I do: I want none of it to have happened. I want my husband back and for him to be the person I always thought he was. I want for him to only have two children: MY two children. I want to be as innocent as I was before he piloted his own plane into the Key of Biscay. Beyond that, I'm not sure it's my place to want or desire anything in particular with regards to his children—all three of them." She swallows around the lump that's forming in her throat. "My girls are grown, and they're going to do whatever they're going to do with that relationship.

My feeling is that they'll be open to letting it grow as Julien gets older, but I have no idea. They have their own emotions to handle when it comes to their father, his choices, and his death."

Dexter stays respectfully silent, but nods as he listens.

"Hi," a man says, approaching with his hands spread to show that he's harmless. It's a stance that a lot of people adopt when they approach Ruby, and it's meant to say, "I have no weapons, I have no camera in hand, and I'm not asking for anything."

Within Ruby's peripheral vision, Banks moves from under the tree and approaches. She gives him a slight shake of the head.

"My wife was just here with our little girl," he says, pointing over to where the young mom is sitting with the toddler fairy in her lap. She waves at Ruby shyly, then holds up her daughter's hand to make her wave as well. "And we don't want to bother you at all, but we both wanted to say that we love you so much, and all that you did for schools and literacy while President Hudson was in office. We're both elementary school teachers," he adds hastily, sounding nervous and excited. "Anyway, we were hoping we could get a picture with you. If not of all of us, then maybe just you with our daughter, Gemma. So she can always have the photo even though she's too young to remember meeting a First Lady."

Ruby smiles and stands, brushing off the seat of her pants. She wants to put this poor guy at ease, as he seems so anxious to ask her for a photo. If she were a betting woman, she'd guess that his wife has put him up to it.

"Of course. I'd love to," she says, smiling at him.

The man waves his wife over excitedly and she jumps up, grabbing Gemma and placing her on one hip so that she can walk quickly over to them before Ruby changes her mind.

"Hi, I'm Beth, and this is Gemma," she says.

"And I'm Dylan," the man adds, realizing that he never said his name.

"Lovely to meet all of you," Ruby says, reaching out to touch the little pink ballet slipper on Gemma's foot. "I can have my friend take the photo," she says, nodding at Dexter. "Do you mind, Dex?"

He stands up and takes Dylan's phone agreeably, waiting while everyone gets into position, with Gemma still on her mother's hip and Ruby in the middle.

"Okay, everyone get ready," Dexter says, holding up the phone and peering at the screen while he gets them in the frame. "One, two, three, say 'pumpkins!'"

"Pumpkins!" they all shout, even Gemma, who giggles and kicks her small feet with glee. She obviously has no idea what all the fuss is about, but she's tickled by the chance to take photos all the same.

Dexter snaps a few more pictures for the happy family, then hands the phone back. Ruby tells them all goodbye and that she's loved meeting them, but inside she feels a wistful nostalgia tugging at her. Dylan and Beth have their whole lives ahead of them, as does baby Gemma. Their little family is just starting to grow and turn into what it will eventually become, and for now, they have nothing but hope, plans, and dreams for their future.

Ruby had all of that once. Her girls were small and their lives ahead were still unknown. Jack was a politician with big plans, and all she knew was the happiness that their lives together brought her. She waves as the family crosses the grass on their way back to their blanket, then looks out at the pumpkins on the water one last time.

"I think this is a good place to break for the night," she says to Dexter, who is still standing next to her. "We can talk more tomorrow."

For tonight, she wants to be alone with her thoughts and her memories. If she can, she wants to fall asleep remembering what it felt like to be a young family without a care in the world. She wants to recall the safety of that moment, and the sense that nothing could unravel the ties that bound them all together.

Because she knows now that those ties aren't nearly as tight as they seem at the beginning, and all it takes is a few wrong choices for them to loosen altogether.

Sunday

The sun has set on Tangier Island, but people are still milling about, standing outside of the tavern on the main drag, walking in and out of the corner grocery store, and trading gossip with one another at the top of the dock. Cameron and Olive have both changed into jeans and sweatshirts with coats, but Sunday is wearing thick corduroy pants, a heavy sweater, and lace-up boots.

"Planning on gutting some fish, Mom?" Olive asks playfully, taking in her outfit from head to toe.

"You never know," Sunday smiles. "You could be called on anytime to help out with a catch of rockfish or speckled trout." She winks at Cameron. "You might mess up your manicure."

"Definitely not," Cameron says, wrinkling her nose. Of the two girls, Cameron is the one least likely to get her hands dirty or to do anything that might be considered even the least bit outdoorsy.

"I love that life on this whole island revolves around the fishing industry," Olive says, watching as three men tie up a boat and step off in their oilcloth coveralls, with boots that come up to their knees. "It's so charming."

Just then, the bells of the church ring loudly to mark that it's seven o'clock.

"Let's go to the Waterfront Restaurant," Sunday says, pointing at a building that looks like a white shack on the water. It has several boats pulled up and docked right at the entrance to the restaurant. "We can get crab cake sandwiches."

They walk in and are immediately hit by the scent of fried fish and onion rings. People are sitting at picnic style tables—some of the men are sitting sideways on the benches, facing one another as they drink glasses of sweet tea or soda—and the music that's playing sounds like 1970s AM radio.

"Do you think they serve Chardonnay by the glass here?" Olive asks, frowning slightly as she scans the room for an empty table. There's one by the window and they wait for a busy looking waitress to point them over to it.

Sunday glances at her daughter as she pulls out a metal chair with vinyl padding that looks like it belongs around a meeting table in an office. "No, babe. I'm sorry, but I might have forgot to mention that Tangier is a dry island."

"Huh?" Olive looks up from the laminated menu that the waitress has placed in her hands. She looks like a little girl who's just been told that there's no dessert.

"You can bring alcohol onto the island and no one is going to search you or anything, but the locals prefer it if you don't. We don't sell it here, there are no bars, and most people don't drink at all."

Cameron is watching and listening to this exchange wordlessly. "So it's like Utah?" she asks.

"Utah isn't totally dry, contrary to popular belief," Sunday says, skimming her own menu as she rests her elbows on the oilcloth table covering; it reminds her of the coveralls that the fishermen were wearing on the dock. "There are about nine cities where you can't purchase liquor in Utah."

"And you know this because?" Cameron stares at her over the top of her menu, which she's holding daintily with just her fingertips as if it might be covered in germs.

"I've been to Utah a number of times. You know I traveled with your father basically everywhere."

"Hmm." Cameron looks back at her menu and says nothing else.

"Oh my sweet heavens!" An older woman with a completely gray bun is approaching their table slowly, her face full of wonder and joy. "Sunday Bellows?"

Sunday stands up slowly, and as she does, recognition dawns. "Miss Williams?"

"Honey, yes!" the woman says, holding out both of her arthritic hands for Sunday to grasp. "I haven't seen you in nearly forty years, but I'd know you anywhere! And I'm not just saying that because you're a famous woman married to a Vice President—you just haven't changed a bit."

"Miss Williams, I would love to introduce you to my daughters. This is Olive, and this is Cameron. Girls, this is Miss Williams, my very favorite teacher ever."

"Oh, Sunday," Miss Williams says, waving a hand and looking flattered. "You're just saying that because none of your other teachers are standing here!"

"No, it's true. You were someone who always believed in me, and I felt that. I loved your class."

"I had your mother in my junior English class," Miss Williams says to Olive and Cameron, her eyes dancing with delight. "She wrote one of the most flawless essays I've ever read from a student, and I taught here on the island for almost fifty years. Your mom is a smart cookie."

"Yikes," Cameron says. "I can't imagine being a teacher for fifty years."

Miss Williams looks at her with amusement. "You would be amazed at how quickly fifty years goes, dear."

"Which essay are you talking about?" Sunday asks, shooting Cameron a warning look.

"The one you wrote about Edgar Allan Poe marrying his first cousin, and how her death drove him to despair and madness, which was reflected so succinctly in stories like *The Tell-Tale Heart*."

Sunday shakes her head as she stands next to their table, looking at Miss Williams, who has to be close to eighty now. "I can't believe you remember that."

"Miss Bellows—or rather, Mrs. Bond—I can't say that you ever forget your star pupils, no matter how far away life takes them. You just hope that the path they're on somehow leads them to the educational opportunities they deserve." She smiles beatifically at Sunday. "And did life lead you to college somewhere?"

Sunday feels her heart sink, because life had not, in fact, deposited her at Georgetown or Princeton or Yale, as Miss Williams so clearly hoped that it had. "Actually, it didn't," she says, trying to hold her head high. "I left Tangier and found my way to D.C., where I worked and lived until I met my husband. Then I became a mother, and now here I am."

Miss Williams' smile doesn't falter in the slightest. "One of life's greatest gifts," she says, looking at Cameron and Olive, "is motherhood. I was never blessed with the chance to raise children, but I would have loved to." She clasps her hands together. "We don't always get what we want though, do we? Instead, we get what we need. For me, that was being a 'school mom' to thousands of children over the course of fifty years. And that was enough."

"You were a wonderful school mom," Sunday assures her, reaching out to take Miss Williams by the hand. "And I'm so happy you came by to say hello. It means the world to me."

The two women embrace in a tight hug, and when Miss Williams finally steps back, there are tears in her blue eyes. "You are a wonder, Sunday Bellows," she says, pulling a Kleenex from the pocket of her cardigan. "It was lovely to meet you young ladies," she says to Olive and Cameron. "You're lucky girls to have the mother you do."

Sunday stands as Miss Williams walks to the door. A woman about half her age is waiting there, holding a coat for the older lady to slip her arms into.

"That's so weird," Olive says, shaking her head. "I never think of you as being in school, Mom. Like, having teachers and going to prom and stuff. Hey, did you go to prom?"

Sunday sits back down at the table and picks up her menu again. "I did not go to prom," she says, shaking her head.

A waitress is standing beside their table holding a notepad, and when they look up at her, they realize that it's not the same waitress who had seated them. "She definitely did not go to prom," the woman says, watching them with tired eyes. "But if she'd stuck around, she could have been the prom queen."

Olive's mouth falls open and Cameron sets her water glass down loudly. "Mom?" she says, looking back and forth between her mother and this stranger, who looks to be about her mom's age, but without the benefit of access to a good hairdresser or up-to-date fashion. "Do you two know each other?"

Sunday sets her menu on the table with a sigh. "Girls, you remember your Aunt Minnie," she says. "Min, your nieces are all grown up."

Minnie puts the pen in her hand behind one ear and looks first at Cameron and then at Olive. After a long minute, her face breaks into a smile that looks like a sunrise cresting over a mountain range. "Well, get over here and give your old Aunt Minnie a hug!" she says, opening her arms wide and waiting for her nieces to stand.

Olive jumps up first, walking right into Minnie's embrace without hesitation. Cameron is a bit more reluctant, but there's a smile on her face like she's happy to be seeing family. Sunday gets up last and hugs her sister, squeezing her quickly and then letting go so that they can stare into one another's faces.

"What the hell are you doing here, girl?" Minnie asks Sunday, leaning against the table with one hand. She looks around and then leans in to Sunday and lowers her voice. "We've got nothing in here but geezers covered in fish guts, and a menu with grease fried in grease. Why don't you come over to my place?"

Sunday looks at her girls with a question in her eyes; they both shrug like they're up for anything. "What time?"

"I'm off in fifteen minutes," Minnie says. "Meet me at home."

Sunday stands and gathers her purse, motioning for the girls to follow. "We'll walk over there now."

"Can't we catch an Uber?" Cameron asks, putting her hand over her stomach protectively.

"Have you seen any cars out there, ding-dong?" Olive says, poking her sister. "It's all bicycles and golf carts."

"Take my cart," Minnie says, fishing a key on a ring with a red disk shaped like a lifesaver out of her pocket. "It's parked out back—the one with the Hudson-Bond bumper sticker on it."

Sunday gives her sister a look that's full of love. "Aww, you didn't."

"Pshaw, girl. Of course I did. You think my sister is gonna end up living in the White House and I'm not gonna put a bumper sticker on my cart to let the world know that I voted to help get her there?"

"Thanks for the vote, Min, but we actually lived at the Naval Observatory in a house there."

Minnie waves this explanation off with a roll of her eyes. "Potato, po-tah-to," she says. "Now head over to my place. Door's unlocked. I'll be there in about twenty minutes."

* * *

The inside of Minnie's house is wood-paneled and warm.

"Mom?" Olive asks, walking around with her hands behind her back as she looks at the photos in the frames on the mantel. "How did you know where Aunt Minnie lived if you haven't been here in almost forty years?"

A slow smile spreads across Sunday's face and she looks at Cameron, who is sitting gingerly on the edge of a couch covered in scratchy plaid fabric. "Because this is the house I lived in my entire life before I left Tangier. I was actually born in the back bedroom," she says, pointing down a hallway. "As were Minnie and our brother Jensen."

Cameron looks surprised. "Seriously? Minnie got the house when your parents died?"

"Sure," Sunday says. "She was here and I wasn't. It's fine—she deserves every single thing my parents had, which I can tell you wasn't much."

The front door opens then, and Olive stops examining every picture in the room. She hurries over to the couch to sit next to her sister.

"Yoo-hoo, I'm home!" Minnie calls out, dropping her purse and kicking off her shoes in the front hallway. She walks into the living room, pulling the sides of her tunic down over her hips as she sighs and stops to stretch her neck from side to side. "So you remembered where

97

the house was, huh?" She winks at Sunday. "Thought you might've forgotten."

"Never."

"You ladies want some hooch?" Minnie walks over to a bookcase, pulls three paperbacks from the shelf, and reveals a flat bottle of Gentleman Jack whiskey that's been hiding behind the books. "I can make you a Jack & Coke?"

"Yes for me," Sunday says quickly, relief coursing through her veins at the thought of alcohol to lubricate this particular visit.

"Okay, yes, please," Olive says, raising a hand like she's in school. She looks at her mom with excitement in her eyes; this trip has obviously defied her expectations of some touristy visit to her mom's hometown, but she's always been game for pretty much anything anyway.

Cameron holds up a hand. "I'm expecting," she says primly, "so no thank you. Just an ice water for me, if you have it."

Minnie looks at Cameron for a second like she must be joking. "What, I look like I don't have running water or ice in my house, girl?"

"No, no," Cameron says, blushing. "It was just a reflex. I didn't mean to make it sound like I thought—"

"Knock it off, Cammy. I'm just yanking your chain." Minnie walks through the front room in just her socks with the bottle of whiskey in one hand. "I'm making three Jack & Cokes and an ice water," she shouts from the kitchen. "I'd tell you to look out the window and keep an eye open for your uncle Ted, but he died three years ago," she adds.

Cameron looks mildly horrified at the casual way Minnie has announced her husband's death. "Mom," she whispers.

Sunday blinks a few times; she and Minnie don't talk a lot, but she can't imagine that it's been more than three years since they've last spoken. She stands up immediately and walks into the kitchen. "Min," she says firmly, forcing her sister to turn and look at her. "Why didn't you call me? Jesus, what happened?" Sunday can feel her eyes filling with tears; she's known Ted Kull her entire life. In fact, Ted and Sunday's high school boyfriend, Irvin, had been first cousins, and she and Minnie had been on countless double-dates with the two boys.

Minnie busies herself with mixing the drinks. "I didn't call for the same reason that you didn't call to tell me you were coming home before you showed up at the Waterfront. Or that you didn't call to let me know that you're going to be a grandma."

"Well, I just found out about the grandma part a few hours ago," Sunday says, wiping her eyes as they stand under the single globe light that hangs above Minnie's chipped enamel kitchen sink. "But I didn't call you because I knew I wouldn't be on this island for more than an hour without you hearing about it anyway."

"EHHHH," Minnie says, sounding like a buzzer in a game show. "Wrong answer. You should have called, Sun."

Sunday's eyes fall to the floor. "And you should have called me when Ted passed. What was it—heart attack?" She cringes at the thought of Ted, sweet as pie Ted Kull, dropping dead on the dock one day after fishing, or maybe just not waking up one morning.

Minnie shakes her head. "Lung cancer. He was diagnosed and then dead in less than six months." Her mouth is pressed in a grim line. "I miss that man every single day."

"Of course you do." Sunday takes the bottle of whiskey from her sister's hands, sets it on the counter, and then puts her arms around Minnie. "I'm so sorry. I truly am."

"I know you are," Minnie says, relaxing into her older sister's arms. They're Irish twins with barely ten months between them, but Sunday is the big sister and always has been. Even her leaving the island was, in a sense, her way of blazing a trail that her younger sister could have followed, had she wanted to. But she'd stayed on Tangier, married Ted Kull, and had Matt and A.J. in quick succession, just as their mother had had them.

Sunday lets Minnie go, and then they finish mixing the drinks and getting Cameron's water so that they can rejoin the girls in the front room.

"Thank you, Aunt Minnie," Olive says gratefully, sipping her Jack & Coke like it's water. "This is perfect."

Minnie laughs. "I don't know that drinking a tacky mixed drink on your old aunt's hand-me-down couch is all that glamorous, girl, but if you think it's 'perfect,' then it most certainly is."

Cameron says nothing, but smiles wanly as she sips her water.

"I brought the girls here for a reason," Sunday says to Minnie, taking the first sip of her own cocktail and letting the whiskey flood through her body.

"I figured."

"I want them to know everything."

Minnie stays quiet. She drinks her Jack & Coke and sways slightly back and forth in the rocking recliner by the front window. "Hmmm," she says, holding her drink in both hands. "That's a lot."

"It is," Sunday agrees. "But I left here in a hurry—"

"You sure as hell did."

"And I never came back."

"That did not go unnoticed," Minnie says sarcastically, but with a smirk. She takes another drink.

"I've talked very little to the girls about my life here, about their grandparents, or about what it was like growing up in this house."

Minnie's chin drops and she looks into her drink as if she's searching for answers there. "Life here was something else," she finally says.

"What was Dad like?" Sunday asks her.

Minnie's eyes fly up to meet her sister's. "You want me to tell this story?"

Sunday nods. "I do."

Minnie clears her throat and rests her head against the back of her recliner as she gazes at the ceiling and formulates her thoughts. "Okay." She lifts her head again and looks at both of her nieces, who are listening intently. "The house you see here now is not the house that your mother and I grew up in. Your uncle Ted and I worked hard to change everything about it after my parents died, and I think we turned this house of horrors into a real home." She glances around the room, her eyes landing on the photographs on the mantel that show Matt and A.J. in various sports attire, holiday photos of Minnie, Ted, and the boys, and posed school photos. "I raised my boys here, and in doing so, I essentially erased some of the bad feelings I had about this place."

Olive's eyes are wide and she's sitting on the edge of the couch, her drink set down on a brown wooden coaster on the coffee table and long forgotten.

Sunday watches her girls, thankful that her sister is willing to tell them a story that she's never been able to tell.

"Anyhow," Minnie goes on, setting her own drink on a small table next to her chair. She folds her hands over her slightly rounded stomach. "When your mom and I were young, we had a brother who you probably know about. Jensen was our parents' pride and joy. He was the oldest, he was a boy, and he loved the water, which endeared him to our father in ways that nothing Sunday and I ever did could do. Jensen and our father went out fishing a lot when he was a boy, and then he joined our dad at fifteen, working long hours on the boat and bringing home the fish that kept our family in a home and with food on the table."

Cameron is listening wordlessly, but Sunday can see on her face that she's taking it all in and calculating as she goes. "Wasn't Jensen sixteen when he died?"

"He was," Minnie confirms, nodding and rocking back and forth in her chair. "He was indeed." She's silent for a moment as the memory of her brother hangs there in the room with her. "Sunday was twelve and I was eleven, and we were waiting for Dad and Jensen to come home one evening, sitting right there in the kitchen at the table as our mom shucked corn for dinner." She points at the round kitchen table with six chairs around it. "But they missed dinnertime, and when someone knocked on the door, you could already feel that it was going to be bad news."

"Who was it?" Olive asks, chewing on her thumbnail.

"It was Officer Mullins," Minnie says. "His kids went to school with us, and you could tell that he wasn't happy to be on our doorstep that night."

The memory of it floods back like a wave knocking Sunday off her feet, and suddenly she's drowning in it. Her eyes fill with tears. "Our mother screamed the minute she opened the door and saw Officer Mullins standing there under the porch light. It was winter. It was cold and raining, but she left the door wide open as she fell to her knees right there." Sunday nods at the entryway, which is only partially visible from the front room. "I remember the chill that blew through the room, and it never left this house after that night."

"No, it did not," Minnie agrees. "Our dad was in the hospital on the mainland, suffering from hypothermia and three cracked ribs from when he hit the side of the boat, but they had no idea where Jensen was."

"I should add that aside from torrential rain, the water was choppy and they probably should have come in an hour sooner than when they tried to turn back, but they got caught in a situation they couldn't control." Sunday's eyes are faraway as she remembers the scene: the hospital with its white sheets, grim nurses, and antiseptic smell. Her mother looking gray and ashen as she sat next to her husband's bedside, purse clasped tightly in her white-knuckled hands.

"They found Jensen the next day," Minnie says, swiping at her eyes. "Our father started drinking immediately, and that's when things went really wrong around here."

"Was Tangier always a dry island?" Cameron asks, clearly caught up in the story.

"It was, but it's not hard to find alcohol if you want it." Minnie shrugs. "Plenty of people bring it right onto the island in coolers, tucked under the fish they catch, and they walk from house to house, making deliveries and collecting cash. You'd be surprised how many wives believe their husbands are abiding by the rules of a dry island, only to find those same husbands out in a workshop, getting tanked on firewater. Our dad didn't even try to hide it, he just told us that what happened in our house stayed in our house, and Sunday and I obeyed, because that's what you did in those days."

"You obeyed, or you paid for it," Sunday adds, looking glassy-eyed.

"And we paid for it," Minnie says, still rocking back and forth rhythmically, as if the motion were soothing her and making the words easier to share. "Our dad had always been a bit emotionally distant from the females in the house, but with alcohol in the mix, he became downright abusive."

Cameron sucks in a sharp breath, and Olive shakes her head in disbelief; their father is and has never been a stellar, hands-on, loving dad, but he's certainly never been abusive. If anything, his absence has always been easily explained away by his political commitments, and they've not only let him off the hook, they've given him credit for his work. Of course, neither girl has ever known anything different, but

Sunday knows that Peter's emotional distance and occasional lack of physical presence has damaged her girls in different ways than her own father's abuse damaged her and Minnie. As with so many daughters, those Daddy issues run deep, and young girls grow into women who end up paying for those issues over and over and in so many ways.

"What happened?" Olive asks, still biting her thumb as she hangs on every word. "What did he do?"

"Oh," Minnie says, turning her eyes to the ceiling again. "He yelled, screamed, shoved, hit with a belt. He pulled our mother's hair and brought her to her knees in the kitchen if he didn't like what she'd made for dinner. He told us girls we were never going to amount to anything, that no man would ever want us, so we'd be stuck cleaning houses and living on government assistance. He told us we weren't smart enough for high school, let alone college, and one time he had a friend over who was as drunk as he was, and when the man put his hands on Sunday in a way that was not appropriate for a grown man to be touching a thirteen-year-old girl, our dad laughed. He did nothing."

Sunday is looking at the floor, burning with rage at the memory. It had happened right here, in this room, and she remembers it now as if it had just happened yesterday. Mr. Dougherty, the man who owned the bait and tackle shop, was drinking whiskey with her father here, in front of the fireplace, when he'd made some joke about Sunday starting to look like she was "ripe for the picking." Sunday had stopped where she was, halfway between the living room and the kitchen, her blood running cold. She'd expected her father to shout at Mr. Dougherty, to throw him out on his ass, maybe even to treat him to a dose of the anger that he regularly treated her and Minnie and their mother to, but instead he'd laughed.

"Sunday's alright," he'd said lazily, nursing both a can of beer and a whiskey from his chair by the window, "but Minnie's going to grow the kind of curves that a man likes to see on a woman. Might as well wait for her to ripen, Bill."

At thirteen, Sunday had only a hazy idea of what was being said about her and her sister, but she'd known it was bad. Very bad. She'd turned around to talk back—something she knew well and good would bring her nothing but trouble, but that she'd been prepared to do anyway—only to find Bill Dougherty standing right behind her. He reached out with both hands and planted them firmly on her hips, pulling her close to him with a sharp yank. Sunday had stumbled, but ended up flat against Mr. Dougherty's chest, his erection pressing against her insistently. He smelled like fishing bait and alcohol, and his body was hot next to hers. She'd nearly vomited.

"I could always sample the older one while I wait for the younger one," Mr. Dougherty said, his breath hot and rancid on Sunday's cheek. "You know what they say: old enough to bleed, old enough to breed—"

"Knock it off, Bill," Sunday's dad had said from his chair, not even bothering to set down his beer to defend his daughter. "Leave her alone. She's just a kid. Still plays with Barbies, for god's sake."

Sunday had yanked away from Bill Dougherty then and hurried through the kitchen, out the back door, and into the summer evening. She'd run and run and run—all around the island and not stopping for breath—and from that night on, she slept with a chair under the knob of her bedroom door, and with her window latched tightly, even in the middle of a hot, muggy summer.

"What the hell..." Cameron looks angry now. She sets her water on a coaster next to Olive's drink and stands up. "I'm glad I never met him."

"You're *lucky* you never met him, babe," Sunday says, watching the fury rise in her daughter. "He died when I was twenty and I didn't even bother to come home."

"No, she did not," Minnie says, sounding accusatory and a little hurt. "Your mother had flown the coop, and never bothered to come back."

"But wait," Cameron says, pacing in front of the fireplace like a detective in a small town crime show, piecing together the puzzle at hand. "If you were thirteen when that happened with your dad and his friend, but you were sixteen when you left the island, what went on during those years?"

"I was seventeen," Sunday confirms. "And in those next four years I avoided home at all costs. I was out from morning until night, going to school, hanging out with friends—"

"And Irvin," Minnie interjects.

"A boyfriend?" Olive looks at her mother for confirmation.

"The boy I loved with all my heart," Sunday says, picturing Irvin in her mind: tall, lanky, curly hair, piercing eyes. "Your uncle Ted's cousin, and the boy I thought I'd be with forever."

"What happened?" Cameron asks, one fist on her hip as she stands next to the mantel. "Did he break your heart?"

"Oh, honey," Minnie says, answering for Sunday. "Life breaks your heart in so many ways that it gets hard to blame any of it on one person or one situation."

Sunday smiles softly. "She's right," she says, feeling tears prickle behind her eyes again. "Life did a number on me with this one."

"What did he do, Mom?" Olive asks. She looks like she's on the verge of sympathetic tears, and Sunday gets up from the chair she's sitting in and walks over to the couch, taking her younger daughter's hand in her own.

"He was a year older than me, Ollie," she says, patting Olive's hand as she holds it. "And he was ready to leave for college."

"Seems pretty typical," Cameron says, sounding unimpressed. "Don't most young people want to leave home as soon as possible and go to college?"

Sunday nods. "That's true," she says. "They do. And Irvin wanted to go more than most—he couldn't wait to get off the island and never see me again."

"Why?" Cameron asks, dropping her chin and looking at her mother as if she's trying to figure out what this younger version of her mother had done to scare off her boyfriend.

With a sad smile filled with regret, Sunday looks right at Cameron and holds her gaze for a beat. "He wanted to leave because there was no future here on Tangier for him. Or rather, the only future for him was one that he didn't want--and I didn't want it, either."

Ruby

It's Ruby's idea to go to the Autumn Bazaar, which is a Christmas Market on the Upper West Side. She meets Dexter at Joe Coffee Company on Columbus Avenue at ten o'clock the next morning, searching for him as she stands outside with Banks nearby.

"Hi, sorry I'm late," Dexter says, approaching her with a huge grin on his face. He looks well-rested and happy to see her, and not for the first time, Ruby thinks about how much he reminds her of Bradley Cooper, with his strong nose and chin, and his high cheekbones dusted with stubble. His wheat-colored hair is blown around a bit, and his chlorine blue eyes are hidden behind a pair of aviator glasses on this bright, sunny morning. "How'd you sleep?"

"Amazingly well, thank you," Ruby says, allowing him to hold the door for her. "And you?"

"Like a rock," Dexter says with a lopsided smile. "And now I'm ready for coffee."

They take their thirteen-dollar espressos to go, wandering through the streets to the market, which is a series of tent-covered tables lined up all along the sidewalks. Some of the streets have been closed to everything but foot traffic, and Ruby leads the way down one of these roads, stopping at booths that sell bushels of apples for making cider, fresh berry and pumpkin pies, and imported lagers from around the world.

"Ooh, apple cider donuts," Dexter says, pointing at a booth that smells like cinnamon and sugar. "Want one? My treat."

Ruby smiles. "Love one." She waits for Dexter on a bench with her coffee in hand, bending forward to pet a small dog in a sweater that wanders over to her as its owner talks to a friend nearby.

"Here you are, milady," Dexter says, handing her a donut in a white paper bag along with a napkin. He sits next to her with his coffee and his own donut. "Shall we people-watch for a while here?"

"We might as well," Ruby says, pulling her donut from the bag and breaking off a big chunk. "Watching other people is one of my favorite pastimes, and I feel like they watch me enough that it's only fair for me to have a turn."

"Sounds reasonable," Dexter says amiably, biting right into his whole donut. "I actually bought an extra donut, so you can share the second one with me if you like." He holds his open bag out to her and she sees a second cider donut nestled there.

"I think one is enough for today," Ruby says, smiling at him happily and licking granules of sugar from her thumb. "But thank you."

They watch people walking by for a bit. When Dexter finally speaks, it's a pointed question. "Any further thought about the email you got from Etienne?"

Ruby had no idea how difficult it would be to "do fun things" while talking about such serious topics. In a way, it might have just been easier for them to hole up in a room together and have discussions that went on all day with only breaks for eating, but she's still glad for the distractions of fall in the city.

"I fell asleep thinking about it, but I have no idea yet what to do, if I'm being honest," she admits. "I'm not going to respond until I've truly formulated a solid thought."

Dexter polishes off his donut and folds the top of his bag so that he can hold it like a handle. "I have a solid thought." He stands up, bag in one hand and to go cup of coffee in the other. "Let's go and browse. I want each of us to pick out one Christmas ornament for the other person, and it has to be something that we think either represents the other person, or that will make them laugh. And the deal is that no matter what we choose, we both have to swear that we'll hang them on our trees this year. What do you say?"

Ruby is still sitting on the bench, looking up at him. She'd barely started to talk about Etienne or how she felt, and this abrupt change of subject surprises her.

"Oh," she says, swallowing her bite of donut. "That sounds fun." And it actually does sound fun, though she feels cautiously guarded about letting herself feel too laid back with Dexter. She's still struggling with how much being around him feels like being around a man she could really enjoy spending time with, and she knows that these are dangerous feelings to have right now.

"Okay," Dexter says, running a hand through his hair as he glances around. "Meet back here in thirty minutes, yeah?"

Ruby laughs. "This is a timed event?"

"Sure. That will put some pressure on us to find something and not to overthink it. This is supposed to be fun."

Ruby stands and wipes her hands on the front of her jeans. She's left her coffee sitting on the bench and she picks it up now, holding it in front of her chest. "I'm in."

Dexter looks at his watch, waits for the second hand to tick around to the top of the clock, and then looks at Ruby. "Ready, set, go."

Without another word, he walks away, still holding his coffee and his donut bag. Ruby watches him go with a smile; at every turn, Dexter surprises her. When she first agreed to this...partnership?—Can she call it a partnership?—she'd been sure that their interactions would feel dry at best, or antagonistic at worst. That she might be too guarded or reserved to ever give him a good story. But then they'd met and everything about Dexter had felt genuinely curious, and like he was truly on her side. Even his more sensitive lines of questioning are gently probing rather than baldly investigative, and it's easy for Ruby to see him for who he is. And, maybe more importantly, to like him for who he is.

Ruby's eyes follow him until he turns a corner and disappears from view. She glances at her watch: 27 minutes to find an ornament for Dexter. Okay, she can do this.

The first booth is all animal-related ornaments: barnyard animals wearing Santa hats; paw prints on clay disks; various types of birds dressed up as wisemen in a manger. Nothing there for Dexter. Ruby moves on. Another booth is comprised entirely of ornaments that look like sexy fruits: a coconut with big red lips and two tiny coconuts attached like breasts; a banana with bedroom eyes; two apples kissing. Not quite right.

Around the corner Ruby finds a booth filled with intricate Christmas train sets. The booth operator has holiday jazz playing from a boombox, and people are slapping credit cards on the counter to pay for eight-hundred dollar purchases like it's nothing. The train sets are amazing, but there's not an ornament in sight. Ruby moves on.

After about twenty-two minutes she finally arrives at a booth that's full of the kinds of holiday decorations she needs. The tent is strung with frosty white lights, and a man with an acoustic guitar is sitting on a stool, strumming a mellow, wordless version of "Last Christmas." She glances around to make sure Dexter isn't lurking over her shoulder, and then picks up a cowboy on a reindeer. His ten-gallon hat is covered in brown glitter, as are his boots. *Not exactly, but getting closer.* She hangs it back on the ornament holder and moves on.

Up by the register is a miniature tree covered in baubles that catch Ruby's eye, so she stops there to browse, glancing at her watch. Three minutes to go. There is a competitive streak that runs through Ruby and it's egging her on here—she can't lose this challenge. It's all in good fun, and there's no prize for "winning," but she still wants to get it right.

Fortunately, as she spins the mini tree, she lands on the perfect ornament and picks it up. Without even looking at the price, she hands it over to the woman working the register, then quickly taps her credit card on the screen to pay for it. With seconds left to spare, she takes her ornament, ignores the fact that there are people in the booth surreptitiously taking video of the former First Lady buying Christmas knick-knacks, and dashes back to the bench where she and Dexter have agreed to meet.

"I'm here! I'm here!" Ruby shouts, holding up her ornament as she approaches.

Dexter looks at his watch with an exaggerated face. "You're thirty seconds late. Should I consider that a forfeit?"

"There's no prize," Ruby laughs, catching her breath. "Only the promise to hang whatever the other person buys on the Christmas tree this year."

"That's true." He sits down on the bench and pats the spot next to him. "Okay, you first."

Ruby sits and hands over the ornament that the cashier has wrapped in tissue paper and put in a bag. "I saw it and for some reason I just knew it had to be yours," she says, watching him hopefully as he starts to remove the white tissue paper. "It's Iceland," she says in a rush, unable to stop herself from explaining. "I thought it was so beautiful."

"It is," Dexter says, holding the round glass ornament in one palm and admiring it. It's green and blue and purple, and the colors bleed together to create the Aurora Borealis in a polar night sky that looks like a painting. "I love it. How did you remember that I love Iceland?"

"Well," Ruby says, tucking her hair behind her ears, "you *did* just tell me yesterday, so I at least had a fighting chance of remembering."

"Thank you," Dexter says, looking touched. "I got this one for you." He hands over a similarly wrapped bag with an ornament inside. "It's Blackbeard," he says as she opens it, watching her hands lift the ceramic pirate on a string from the paper.

Ruby's smile is enormous as she realizes that he's gotten her a pirate ornament for her first Christmas on Shipwreck Key. It's perfect.

"He's got real yarn for a beard," Dexter adds.

Ruby runs her fingers over the little twists of dark brown yarn that make up his beard. The pirate is holding a gun in one hand a sword in the other, and his mouth is wide open as if he's been caught mid-action, shouting "Ahoy, matey!" at an oncoming foe. His ceramic jacket is flapping in the wind, and he looks fearsome.

"I love it!" Ruby says, looking at Dexter with shining eyes. She truly does love it, because it shows how much thought he put into it. She felt a bit like Blackbeard when she swept onto Shipwreck Key with the wind blowing her hair around, guns drawn, ready for action. And okay, maybe she wasn't there for battle, per se, but she was there to carve out her own future in an unknown land. "I will hang it on my tree with pride," she says, beaming as she re-wraps the ornament and puts it into her purse.

They spend the afternoon wandering the bazaar, looking at Christmas stuff in October, and listening to holiday music under the bright autumn sun. Throughout the day, Dexter pulls more stories from her as they stop to laugh at a grumpy looking cat on a leash wearing an elf costume, and against Dexter's will, Ruby gets him to pose with her in Santa's workshop, where they both kneel next to the Big Man in Red while wearing silly, hand-knitted stocking caps with tassels.

It's a fabulously weird and unexpected day, and Ruby loves every minute of it. She loves it so much that she knows she needs to be on the next plane out of New York City, otherwise she's going to do something rash and somehow reveal to Dexter how much she feels like a woman again in his presence—not just a female, but a *woman*. She's on a slippery slope here, and she needs to find more secure footing fast.

Dexter is surprised and visibly disappointed when she tells him that she needs to get back to Shipwreck Key as soon as possible to handle some things there, but she holds firm, even turning down his invitation to dinner that night. She knows that this project is too important to both of them now to muddy the water with longing or romantic feelings, and she's going to stick to her guns on this one—just like Blackbeard holding Charleston for ransom until his requests for medicine were met, only with a lot less violence than the most notorious pirate in history.

The very next day, Ruby is on a plane, flying high over the Eastern Seaboard towards home, with her ceramic pirate ornament tucked safely inside the purse that's resting on her lap. She breathes a sigh of relief at every mile that she puts between herself and Dexter North.

It's better this way, she tells herself, watching the Atlantic Ocean far below from her seat by the window. *I need to stay clear-headed for this book. I need to tell my story. I need to figure out my life.*

But a little part of her misses Dexter's smile. She misses the way he cracks a joke or says something sly and then looks at her, waiting for her to pick up on it. She misses the way he asks questions and then really

listens to her answers. She misses the way he can go from a serious journalist to a silly guy who wants to buy her a Christmas ornament in the
blink of an eye.

But mostly, she misses the way he makes her feel, and *that* is the
reason that she's on an airplane, winging her way home instead of sitting
across from Dexter at a coffee shop, staring into his blue, blue eyes.

Sunday

The evening with Minnie was enlightening for Cameron and Olive, if Sunday is judging by their faces and the questions they asked, but Minnie had stopped short of revealing the real catalyst for Sunday's departure from Tangier almost forty years earlier, and she knows that the time has come to take her girls right to the source.

"Where are we going?" Olive asks from the back seat of the golf cart that Minnie has kindly loaned them for the day. She's agreed to walk wherever she needs to go or to hitch a ride from a neighbor, and Sunday appreciates this small kindness.

"Here," Sunday says, pulling the cart over to the side of the road and parking in gravel. She turns off the power and leaves the key in the ignition. Tangier is a classic small town where front doors don't need to be locked, and a golf cart with a key left dangling in the ignition isn't going anywhere. "It's time for me to talk to someone, and I'd like for you to be with me when I do."

Cameron looks dubious, and Olive's eyes grow serious. "Mom, are you in some sort of trouble?" She looks at the weather-beaten house that they've parked in front of. "Does someone you don't get along with live here?"

Sunday shakes her head and takes a deep, fortifying breath. "No.

Remember how I told you last night about my high school boyfriend, Irvin?" The girls watch her but say nothing. "This is where he lived. His mother is still here."

Minnie had assured her on her way out the door the night before that she'd find Mavis Kull, Irvin's mother, still living here. The woman has to be nearly as old as Miss Williams, her former teacher, but she's living in the house alone, with nothing but a little dog and daily food deliveries from the local, makeshift version of Meals on Wheels that helps out the elder islanders and those who are housebound due to various disabilities.

Sunday walks ahead of the girls, determined not to lose her nerve. She knocks on the door loudly, hoping that she won't scare Mrs. Kull, but that she'll rouse her from her recliner and her daytime television, which she can see flickering through the window that looks into the front room.

A woman so old and wrinkled opens the door that Sunday nearly does a double-take; Mavis Kull had been a short, muscular whip of a woman with steely eyes and a sharp tongue when Sunday had dated her son. Now she's wizened and shrunken, and she looks at Sunday without recognition.

"Mrs. Kull?" Sunday asks, stepping back politely so that the screen door still separates them. Olive and Cameron stand behind her, and she can feel their nervous energy the same way she can smell the salty air of the bay all around her. "It's Sunday Bellows. I don't know if you remember me—"

Mrs. Kull reaches forward and unlatches the screen door. "What are you, some kind of idiot, Sunday Bellows? Of course I remember you. Now get in here before you let all my warm air out."

Sunday steps through the door, as she's been directed to do. "These are my daughters, Mrs. Kull. This is Cameron, and Olive."

"They don't look a whole helluva lot like either you or your good for nothing husband," Mrs. Kull remarks, looking each of the girls up and down. "Don't care for your husband's politics a whole lot, and I sure don't like the looks of him—he's a bit shifty for my taste."

Sunday bites her tongue, holding back her comments about Mr. Kull, who was well known as the island cad, having had reported flings with women Sunday had admired greatly, like Miss Williams, and also Dr. Pembroke, the island's only doctor and a woman who had done her medical training at Harvard. No one knew what it was that Bob Kull had to offer all of the women who flocked to him, but it's none of Sunday's business and the man has been dead for at least twenty-five years, so none of it really matters now.

"We're divorcing," Sunday says flatly, hoping to end the discussion of Mrs. Kull's dislike for Peter.

"Sounds about right," Mrs. Kull says with obvious distaste. "You always were a runner."

"May we sit down?" Sunday asks, looking at the couch across from Mrs. Kull's reclining chair. "We won't stay long."

"Might as well sit. But my program comes on in thirty minutes, so let's make a point rather than just talking about the weather." Mrs. Kull lowers herself slowly into her reclining chair and her dirty pink slippers rise off the ground as she moves the handle to lift her feet and extend them.

"I wanted to apologize," Sunday says quickly, sitting on the three-person couch with her daughters on either side of her. They are silent and she can feel their uncertainty as they wait to see where this conversation goes. "I left and never gave anyone the chance to do... anything."

"Damn straight," Mrs. Kull says, staring at her with a gaze that could bore holes in a steel door. "You left and my Irvin was heartbroken. Wasn't fair at all, if you ask me."

Sunday swallows and takes a moment to gather her thoughts. "I didn't ask you, and that was intentional. I left Tangier because I was afraid you and my mother and any number of other people would have tried to convince me to stay. And I thought that maybe Irvin would try to stay here instead of going to college, and that's not what you wanted him to do, is it?"

Mrs. Kull finally averts her gaze, moving her dentures around in her mouth as she looks at her muted television stubbornly.

Next to Sunday, Olive coughs lightly into her hand.

"I left so that your son could do what he needed to do, and so that I could do what I needed to do, because I didn't believe that a seventeen-year-old girl should have to give up her own hopes and dreams just because of one mistake."

Mrs. Kull huffs angrily. "Mistake, my ass," she mutters. "A child isn't a mistake."

Cameron gives a small gasp of recognition. "Mom, you were *pregnant*?"

Sunday turns to look her daughter in the eye. "I was," she admits. "I was pregnant, and I wanted to give my child a far better life than the one I could have given him here on Tangier Island. I wanted him to have the kind of life that your little one is going to have, Cam. A life with educated parents, with the promise of travel and success and a future. I knew I could never give him that if Irvin and I had had the baby ourselves and tried to make a go of it."

"Your parents would have let you live with them, Sunday Bellows, you know they would have," Mrs. Kull says forcefully. "Or you could have married my son and I would have put you up here until you could get your feet under you."

"Nope. Not an option, Mrs. Kull. My house was filled with anger and contempt, and your house wasn't entirely stable either." It's all she's going to say on the matter, but she can tell by the wilting look in Mavis Kull's eyes that she's hit a nerve; Mavis knows that she's referring to her husband's comings and goings. "How is Irvin doing these days?" Sunday asks, switching tacks smoothly so that she can prove her point.

Mrs. Kull capitulates. "He's living in Maine with his wife and their three children. Irv is a dentist."

"Do you think he would have been as successful if he'd stayed here and been a teen dad?"

"At least he would have been here. Now that Bob is dead and Irv moved off-island, I'm all alone," Mrs. Kull says bitterly. "And my grandchild is out there somewhere in the world, I assume, unless you..." Her face takes on a horror-stricken expression, as if the thought just occurred to her, forty years after the fact, that Sunday might have chosen *not* to give birth and put the baby up for adoption.

Sunday doesn't leave her in suspense. "Mrs. Kull, your grandson is out there in the world—at least as far as I know. I was able to have him and choose a family myself, and I picked the very best people I could."

Mavis Kull looks unimpressed, but she's listening. "I chose a couple who were both scientists with degrees from Johns Hopkins, and they couldn't have kids themselves." Her eyes tear up at the memory—she hasn't cried as much as she's cried in the past couple of days in years. "When I said goodbye to the baby at the hospital, they let me know that they were naming him Benjamin, and I've held that close to my heart all these years." She puts a hand to her chest and lets the tears fall. "Benjamin is out there somewhere, and while I may never meet him, I do think I gave him the life he was supposed to have, and it wasn't here on Tangier."

"Huh." Mrs. Kull closes her mouth tightly and her jaw clenches. "You still didn't give any of us a say in what happened to him, but I guess I appreciate the apology after all these years."

"Mrs. Kull," Sunday says, scooting forward on the couch and making eye contact with the old woman. "The apology is for leaving without telling you all what my decision was, but it was *my* decision to make, and I'm not sorry that I didn't let you all make the choice for me. I've had a wonderful and interesting life—one I never could have had here on this island—and I have to believe that Benjamin has as well."

Mrs. Kull drops the handle on her chair and her feet swing back to the floor, letting Sunday know that she's worn out her welcome. She stands, and Olive and Cameron quickly follow suit.

"Thank you for letting us come in to talk, and if you think it's a wise choice, I hope you'll give Irvin my best. I think he'd agree with me that we both ended up having the lives that we were supposed to have, and I don't think you'd trade in the three grandchildren he's given you, even if they do live in Maine."

Sunday walks to the door and then turns around to see Mrs. Kull still sitting in her chair. "We'll show ourselves out, and again, thank you for letting me say my piece."

Without waiting for Mavis Kull to respond, Sunday and her daughters walk back out into the October afternoon, closing the door to the old house and letting the screen door slam shut behind them.

* * *

"So you were pregnant at seventeen?" Olive is sitting on one side of Sunday at the edge of an old, unused dock, and Cameron is sitting on the other. Their legs dangle over the water, and they watch as boats drift past, coming and going from the newer dock down the island.

Sunday nods and squints out at the horizon. The morning is bright and slightly overcast, and there is the distinct smell of autumn in the air: bonfires and fallen leaves, with tang of colder air in her nostrils. Sunday breathes it all in, then releases it.

"I was. And I didn't want to make the same mistakes my own mother did. She couldn't have known she'd end up married to a man who was drunk and abusive—certainly it didn't start out that way—but to stay on an island with a baby and no chance of leaving to get an education couldn't have ever ended up the way I wanted my life to go."

"Will you tell us what happened when you left here?" Cameron asks, and for the first time in as long as she can remember, Sunday doesn't hear judgment or acrimony in her older daughter's tone.

"I didn't tell my parents I was pregnant. I told Minnie and I told Irvin, but telling two teenagers is as good as telling the world, so I knew that as soon as I left, word would get out. But I didn't care, because by then I knew I'd be on the mainland and on my way to wherever I was going."

"Where did you go?" Olive asks, lacing her fingers through Sunday's and holding her hand supportively. She looks appalled at the thought of a seventeen-year-old pregnant girl let loose in the world.

"I went straight to Washington D.C. because in my mind, that was the center of the universe, and that was where I'd have the best chance of getting lost and finding my own way. But first, I had to have the baby. So I found a place—we used to call them 'homes for unwed mothers'—and they agreed to let me live there until my baby was born, with the under-standing that I'd give him up for adoption at birth."

The girls both look confused at the idea of a dormitory for girls with big, round bellies and no man to stand by their side as they gestated and birthed their babies. In their relatively short lifetimes, women have always had the right to choose their own paths: women can have their babies or not, keep them or give them up, raise them alone or rely on family who accepts the new addition to the family without the shame that used to be attached to teenage pregnancies. Things were different when Sunday was young.

"What was it like?" Olive asks.

Sunday thinks back to her time there. It was a two-story house in the suburbs, run by a group of nuns from a local church who didn't wear habits, but instead dressed in cardigans and button-up blouses. They kept their hair and nails short, and their adornment minimal. If they wore jewelry at all, it was a simple cross around the neck or a band around the ring finger. The decor was as sparse as the nuns' appearances: simple dining table and chairs; plain beige couches; two single beds to a room with nothing but a nightstand and lamp between them. You worked a job in the small town while pregnant, gave a portion of your paycheck to the church to help pay the bills of the house and buy the communal food, and then you gave birth and moved out with the money in the bank from the job you'd been working. It was a well-honed system, and a peaceful time in Sunday's life. She'd loved being pregnant, and the other girls in the house were quiet and obedient, just as she was.

"It was nice," she says now to her girls. "We had rules and chores and bedtimes, and there was no upheaval. I made friends with a few of the girls, and we'd sit outside in the summer, playing cards after dinner. There was a small library two blocks from the house, and I think I read every *Sweet Valley High* book they had."

"What's *Sweet Valley High*?" Cameron frowns.

Sunday pats her daughter's thigh with the hand that's not holding Olive's. "It's the sign of a generation gap, babe." She laughs softly. "Anyhow, I read books and worked in an ice cream shop, and when Benjamin was born, I had about two thousand dollars in the bank. The nuns let me stay in the house for a few more nights after I gave birth just to get my strength back, and then I took my two thousand dollars and found an apartment in D.C. with Rennie, another girl who'd lived in the house with me and had just had her baby. I got a job in a coffee shop, signed up for classes at the College of Southern Maryland, and got my two-year degree. Then I just got on with it. By the time I was twenty-two, I was married to your father."

Cameron is rubbing her belly absentmindedly, though there's no visible bump there yet. "But...do you ever really 'get on with it'? Like, how does a person give away their child and then just wake up the next day and keep living?"

Sunday thinks about how to answer this. "I think that everyone probably has their own ways of coping. For me, I knew I was doing the right thing for myself, for Irvin, and for the baby. It would have never worked for us to stay on Tangier. Or rather, it would have, but it wouldn't have been the best situation for any of us. So I did what I knew I needed to do."

"Did you ever regret it?" Olive asks, still holding her mother's hand.

"Sure. Of course. I regretted it in the sense that I never got to know my son, but I didn't regret it in the sense that I wish I'd done things differently. I accepted that I wanted him to have a better life, and then I had nine months to mentally prepare myself for letting him go."

"How was it the day you had him?" Cameron asks. "When you had to hand him over to strangers knowing you'd never see him again?"

"Hard," Sunday says honestly. "The hardest thing I've ever gone through in my life before or since. I think about him everyday—even all these years later. But I knew I'd chosen well and that he'd be loved, and that's really all anyone can ask for in that situation." Sunday pauses. "I would imagine that your parents felt the same way," she says, looking in turn at each of her girls, and wondering for the millionth time what might have possessed their own parents to put them both up for adoption.

"I don't think my parents wanted me," Cameron says as she stares at the water. Sunday looks at her profile and watches the way Cameron holds her shoulders straight and tries to be tough. "I bet their families didn't want me, either." She turns to look at Sunday, then lifts her chin vaguely in the direction of Mavis Kull's house. "But you both had family who would have taken Benjamin or helped you to raise him. Do you feel bad knowing that he might be out there thinking the same things I think? That no one loved or wanted him?" Her words sound harsh, but her tone is searching, and Sunday knows that Cameron isn't trying to hurt her.

"Sure, babe. I've wondered that. Of course. But I'd like to believe that his life has been so good that I'm nothing but a passing thought—if he thinks of me at all. I'd be totally fine if he never did. If he'd blended in so seamlessly to his new family that I vanished into the background. That would be the best case scenario. I don't need to believe that I have a child out there, pining for his birth mother." She bites her lower lip and watches a fishing boat pass by with three men on it, all decked out in coveralls and with hats on their heads. One lifts his cap in Sunday's direction and she gives a half-hearted wave. "Do either of you pine for your birth mothers?" Sunday asks the question, but even as she does, she's afraid of the answer.

"No," Cameron says quickly. "Never."

Olive shrugs and watches the boat as it moves out into the open water. "Sometimes," she admits. She turns to Sunday quickly. "I'm sorry, Mom. I don't mean to make you feel bad, I just wonder about her. And about the rest of the family I never knew."

"Oh, love, of course you do." Sunday squeezes Olive's hand reassuringly. "I don't fault you for that. And I want you both to know that if you ever want to seek out your birth families, I'll move heaven and earth to help you find them."

Simultaneously, as if they'd planned it, Olive and Cameron lean into their mother, placing their heads on both of her shoulders. She smiles as tears spring to her eyes.

"You know," she says, wrapping an arm around each of her girls. "I wanted you both to come here with me because I think it's high time you know where I really come from. But also because your dad has threatened to tell my story for me, and I don't think that's his right."

"It's not," Olive agrees, leaving her head on Sunday's shoulder. "I'm going to tell him not to."

"That won't stop him," Cameron says, lifting her head to look around Sunday at her sister. "You know he does whatever he wants."

The three women are silent as they contemplate this, and Sunday knows that her girls are well aware of all of Peter's rumored indiscretions. She just hopes they have no clue about the finer points of his bad behavior, like getting caught in the kitchen pantry at the White House with Adam the chef.

"I guess I wanted to bring you here and tell you all this myself so that he couldn't beat me to the punch," Sunday explains. "He's going to do whatever he's going to do in the press, and he's going to reveal my life and my story to make himself look better, but I don't really care what a bunch of strangers thinks about me anyway. The only two people in the world who I want to *really* know me and understand me are you two girls. And I hope now that you do."

"I think I understand you...better," Cameron says slowly.

Olive lifts her head from Sunday's shoulder. "Me too."

"I can see now that you married Dad when you were still pretty young, and that you fought hard for the life you ended up with. And that maybe you didn't want to let go of that life just because he wasn't the perfect husband."

Sunday nearly snorts at the words "perfect husband" being used in the same sentence as Peter, but she doesn't. "That's true, honey." She puts a hand on Cameron's back and rubs in slow circles. "I had you girls to think about, and frankly, I knew what I *didn't* want my family to be. I wanted to give you everything I could, and to be the best mom I could be. But don't forget as you start your own journey into motherhood, Cam, that it's hard work. And you will make mistakes. As long as you do everything with love, then that's the most you can ask for. And everything I've done—every choice I've made—is out of love for you two girls."

"Mom, can I ask one more question?" Olive says.

"Sure, babe."

"Why did you adopt us instead of having more kids of your own? Was it because you felt bad about Benjamin?"

Sunday is gobsmacked for a second, and she doesn't answer right away. "I think I felt like someone out there in the world was raising my baby and giving him a better life than I ever could have, and that I knew I could do the same for some other woman—I could raise her baby and be the mother that she couldn't be at that moment."

Cameron nods, digesting this. "That makes sense." She stops talking and stares at her mom meaningfully. "I'm glad you did. I'm glad you're my mom."

"Me too," Olive says, kissing Sunday on the cheek. "Me too, Mama."

Ruby

"Girls, girls, settle in," Ruby says, waving at the chairs she's set up in the back room of Marooned With a Book. "We've got a ton of stuff to talk about."

"And I bet it's not even about the book," Molly says, biting into a lemon poppyseed scone that she's brought over from The Scuttlebutt to add to the hasty smorgasbord they've made this week for book club. Gone are the formalities of the first couple of meetings, with the carefully prepped snacks, the proper voting on books to read and discuss, and the getting-to-know-you awkwardness, and in their place are random bites to eat, a system of suggesting whatever sounds good to read and then voting by raised hand, and a growing familiarity that feels deeply comforting to Ruby.

The table at the side of the room is laden with cheese and crackers, Molly's scones, some onion dip and a bag of chips, a platter of fruit, and three different kinds of wine. Ruby has also set out a pot of hot water and a variety of teabags for anyone not wanting wine, but this evening every woman has a glass of wine in her hand except for Tilly, who, at nineteen, is drinking a can of Coke.

"It's not about the book," Sunday confirms, crossing her legs and biting into a cracker and a hunk of smoked gouda. "We've both got stories from our far-flung travels."

"You first," Ruby tells her, sitting down with a small paper plate loaded with snacks in one hand and a clear plastic cup of red wine in the other. "Tell us about Tangier Island."

Ruby and Sunday have already pulled an all-nighter since being back on Shipwreck Key, and they've talked about everything that happened on their respective trips. Harlow and Athena had been there as well when they built a huge fire in Ruby's fireplace and settled in with blankets and mugs of tea to talk, but these other women have become their support network—their friends—and they want to bring them up to date and share their stories with Heather, Marigold, Molly, Vanessa, and Tilly, too.

"Okay, where do I start..." Sunday pours herself another half glass of wine and sighs, thinking of the quick trip back to her childhood home. "First of all, as I told you, Cameron didn't want to go, but she agreed to meet us in Virginia, and we all got on the ferry together."

"Good thing she showed, or I would have called her myself," Molly grouses.

"No, she showed. And they got to see the island, my sister Minnie, the house we grew up in, and they even met my favorite teacher."

The women are all listening quietly, waiting for the big reveal. Sunday doesn't want to keep them in suspense for too long, or drag them on with stories about rusty boats, the peculiar accent of the locals, or the pervasive smell of fish on Tangier Island, so she cuts to the chase. "They also heard about my brother's death, my dad's drinking and how abusive he got, and about how I got pregnant at seventeen and ran away from home for good."

All sound has been sucked out of the room by this revelation, and when Sunday looks at the other women, she sees that they're holding their collective breath as they wait for more.

"I got pregnant by my high school boyfriend, Irvin, and I knew right away that I didn't want to take away his chance to leave the island for college, or take away my own chance at a future that was far bigger than anything I would have on Tangier. I also knew that whatever life we could offer a baby was nothing compared to what a family with more education, more life experience, and more means could do."

"That's brave," Molly says softly, giving Sunday an encouraging nod.

"It was simply what I had to do. And on this trip, I realized that adopting my girls was my way of turning around and doing the same thing for another woman's baby, giving it a home and a life and all the love that she—for whatever reason—couldn't."

The women are quiet and awed. Ruby is sitting next to Sunday and she reaches for her hand.

Sunday looks down at her lap. "It's a huge part of my heart, and of who I am as a woman and a mother."

"Do you think you'll ever try to find the baby?" Heather asks, the plate in her lap ignored as she takes in the enormity of this story.

"Benjamin," Sunday says, looking up to meet her eyes. "It was a boy, and they let me hold him, and told me that they were naming him Benjamin. And no, I wouldn't go in search of him, but all these years I've been aware that he might come searching for me, and I would welcome it if he did."

Heather stands up first. "Could I propose our very first group hug?" she asks, holding her arms wide. "If you're not comfortable with it, don't feel like you have to join, but I think that there are times when we just need to physically feel our friends wrapping around us, and this is one of those times."

Ruby stands and helps Sunday to her feet, followed by Marigold, Harlow and Athena, Vanessa, Molly (somewhat reluctantly), and finally Tilly, who rolls her eyes so far back in her head that she looks like she no longer has irises. The women come together, at first a bit awkwardly, wrapping their arms around whoever is next to them. After the initial figuring and reconfiguring, they're in a loose version of a group hug and the laughter starts. First, it's Ruby, laughing because she's somehow in the middle of the huddle next to Sunday. But then it spreads, and soon they're all giggling.

"I haven't even told you about Dexter yet!" Ruby shouts from the middle of the hug. "Should I just do that while we're already standing here so that you all can support me when I keel over?"

"No!" Heather shouts, pulling away from the group. "No, no, no! Everyone gets their own group hug when they need it." She plops down in her chair and the other women go back to their seats.

"Alright," Molly says, "we've talked babies and kids, so now let's talk men."

Harlow and Athena make eye contact nervously, and Ruby catches it; she doesn't want to upset her daughters by talking about a man other than Jack, but she recalls a book club meeting where Harlow very clearly stood in support of Ruby being able to live her own life going forward. Besides, the girls are old enough now to know that their mother isn't going to (most likely) be a single woman entrenched in widowhood forever.

"Okay," Ruby says, inhaling deeply through her nose and then breathing out as she sits, crosses one leg over the other, and straightens her spine. "First of all, New York was amazing. The weather was so beautiful, and we went to Fort Tryon Park—"

"But did you get down and dirty?" Marigold asks, holding her wine like she's about to take a celebratory sip. Her eyes are dancing beneath her dark brows, and she tosses her loose hair back over one shoulder. "Tell us the good stuff, please."

Ruby blows out a long breath and slumps back in her chair. "I came home early."

"What? No! Why?" came the various shouts as the other women sit forward in their seats, waiting for more.

"Did he do something wrong?" Molly asks, shaking her head with a look on her face that says she'd expect nothing less from a man.

"No, god—no. It wasn't him at all," Ruby says, waving a hand back and forth. "Nothing like that. In fact, we went out and did fun things all over the city: we ate outside, sat in the park and looked at the fall leaves, went to a pumpkin flotilla at night, and then to a Christmas bazaar in the morning, it's just..." Ruby pauses, picking at her cuticles as she considers how to phrase her feelings. "It was *too* nice. I mean, we talked about serious stuff, which is always the goal for our face-to-face meetings, but we also had that really good, easy conversation that you have, you know..."

"When you're catching feelings for someone," Athena offers, looking a little sad. Ruby looks at her older daughter and remembers how hard she'd fallen for a guy named Diego who she worked with at the Library of Congress, and how the subsequent heartbreak had brought her to Shipwreck Key.

Ruby gives her daughter a private smile. "Exactly," she confirms. "When we're together, I sometimes forget that we're actually supposed to be working. It starts to feel..."

"Like a date," Marigold finishes for her, giving a knowing nod. "I know those kind of relationships, and they're hard to define."

"Do you think he feels the same way?" Heather asks hopefully. "You two would be really good together."

Ruby laughs dryly. "Well. I don't know about that. And I have no idea if he feels the same way," she says, omitting the conversation they'd had at Fort Tryon Park where he admitted to being less than impartial about her. "But I do know that looking at him and thinking about whether or not he's a good kisser is a fast way to derail this book project."

"Ooooh!" Vanessa, normally quiet and more of an observer, bounces in her seat. "I love that. It's so romantic. The two of you, strolling through the park and talking about your lives—it's just so perfect."

Everyone turns to Vanessa, watching as her eyes dance with the image of love blooming under the autumn sun in New York City. Ruby knows that Vanessa wants nothing more than to live the fantasy of true love, a happy marriage, and a beautiful family, but she's living on an island where the prospects for love are minimal, at best, and as a fuller-figured girl with a quiet nature and a love of books, she has a hard time putting herself out there. There's a sweetness and a naïveté to Vanessa that makes her entirely lovable.

"He's something else," Ruby allows. "Obviously good looking, smart, curious, and with depth, but...aside from the fact that we're working on a professional project, there's also the small matter of our vast age difference." She can't even bring herself to look at either of her daughters; the idea of their disapproval is more than she can bear.

Molly scoffs—a loud, disbelieving huff. "Come on, Ruby. That's not real."

"What's not real?" Ruby blinks in surprise.

"That a smart accomplished woman like yourself is going to fall for that kind of mumbo-jumbo. 'Age gap,' my arse."

Marigold cackles loudly. "Preach, sister!"

"I'm serious," Molly goes on, brow furrowed and face set in disbelief. "You're both grown adults with a wealth of life experience between you. Who cares about a few years this way or that? It's nonsense. It's an excuse. If the two of you don't care about it, then it's nobody else's business. They're certainly allowed to speculate, but if they do, it's most likely because they're jealous."

"I can speak to that," Heather says, raising a hand and looking a little shy. "I have some experience with age gap romances."

Ruby turns to her, ready to hear Heather out. "And what's the biggest age gap you've had in a relationship?"

Heather screws up her face as she does the math. "Husband number two: forty-one years."

Marigold hoots. "That's not just a tiny little valley of an age gap, that's the Grand Canyon!"

Heather lifts her eyebrows like she doesn't care. "It was. But I loved him."

Molly gives her a stern look—not disapproving, just serious. "What did you love most about him?"

"I was twenty-five and he was sixty-six when we fell in love. He'd seen things I couldn't even dream of—"

"Like the Great Depression?" Marigold teases.

The corner of Heather's mouth lifts in a half-smile. "More like life stuff. He already knew how to navigate the world, and I learned from him. And he'd been in love—more than once—so I knew that he was capable of it. He was a father, and I got to see how much he loved his children. He was old enough that he wasn't always in a hurry, so he was patient. And he listened a lot because he'd already figured out that the person who talks the most is the one who has the most to learn, not the most to teach. I liked everything about him, and his age was probably the last thing that worried me."

Everyone turns to Ruby to see her reaction. "Okay, so we're talking more like thirteen years and not forty-one, and this discussion is actually making me feel a little ridiculous, because it's not like I'm old enough to be his mother or anything."

"Good," Molly says, nodding. "You *should* feel ridiculous, because you're making a mountain out of a molehill. Now, when are you seeing him again?"

"I told him I needed to get back here to handle a few things, and we agreed to Zoom in a week or so. I don't think he was offended that I left early, but he might have been a little puzzled. I don't know. I'm just not sure how to proceed without—" She turns to Athena, "Wait, what was I doing?"

"Catching feelings," Athena, Harlow, and Tilly all say in unison.

"Right."

"So what if you do catch these feelings?" Molly folds her arms over her chest and drops her chin as she observes Ruby. "Life is about feelings and relationships and emotions. That's showbiz, baby."

There's something hilarious about the way that Molly, with her short, unruly, graying hair, thick sweatshirt, worn-in 501s, and filed down, unpolished nails is doling out relationship advice that makes far more sense than anything that's going on in Ruby's head. Without warning, Ruby breaks out in a laugh.

"Molly," she says, shaking her head, "you are so right. I need to be less afraid of stuff like this, because I've still got a lot of life ahead of me." Ruby grows serious again. "But I do need to make sure I don't get carried away and undo all of our hard work so far on the book."

"Sure, kiddo. Tell yourself whatever you gotta tell yourself to get through the night," Molly says, settling back in her chair with a knowing smile. "And can someone pass the wine? I'm gonna need a refill if we're still going to talk about the book."

But they don't ever get around to the book, because Marigold wants to know more about Heather's husbands, and Molly starts telling them funny stories about how her late husband, Rodney, used to fart like a foghorn in his sleep and how much she misses it, and Sunday worries with them about what Peter will do next now that she's told her daughters about the baby she put up for adoption. Ruby starts to realize that between the secrets, the stories, and the group hugs, what she really has there in her shop on that dark October evening is not just a book club, but a group of friends—real, supportive, loving friends.

Marooned With a Book has truly come to life for her, and this place, these women—they've become her home. Ruby smiles at them all with shining eyes.

Dexter

Theo Harris walks into Dwell at eight o'clock on the dot. Dexter has chosen the popular bar in the basement of an old garment factory, and as Theo pauses in the doorway, looks around, then lifts his goateed chin in recognition at his old friend, Dexter smiles. He knows that Theo will appreciate the Englishness of this particular bar, with its dark leather banquettes, wooden beams running the length of the low ceiling, intimate wall sconces at each booth, and the selection of imported whiskeys.

"Mate," Theo says, throwing his arms around Dexter and pounding his back as Dexter stands to greet his London-based buddy. "So glad we could meet up while I'm in town."

"Same," Dexter says, sliding back into the booth. Theo tosses his jacket and a leather bag onto the bench on the opposite side of the table and slides in across from Dexter. "Should we get a couple of steaks and catch up?"

"Can we start with a drink?"

Dexter lifts his nearly empty glass. "I started without you."

"Then let me catch up." Theo lifts a finger at a passing server and asks for another round for Dexter and one for himself. "Okay, now that we've got that sorted, let's talk business and women, but not necessarily in that order."

Dexter runs a hand through his hair and laughs at Theo's rakish grin; his old friend is an incorrigible flirt and always has been. The men had attended Oxford together fifteen years prior, and Dexter remembers being in awe of how women flocked to Theo, with his handsome male model face and his devilish laugh and sense of humor. It hadn't surprised him at all when Theo had gotten hired on at the BBC and been made a foreign correspondent, but it had made it more difficult for the old friends to meet up and have a drink.

"I'm afraid my business and my women are overlapping at this point," Dexter says, rolling up the sleeves of his well-worn denim button-up shirt and pushing them to his elbows. He sits back in the booth and lifts his whiskey glass. "So you go first. Tell me what you got for work, then tell me how many women you're currently promising to make the future Mrs. Harris."

Theo makes a face. "I've decided that there will never be a Mrs. Harris other than my mum. I'm done with women." He knocks back his first sip of whiskey and pulls a different face than the one he'd made thinking about marriage. "That's good," he says, setting the glass on the table.

"Huh," Dexter says, trying to stifle his amusement.

Theo holds up a hand. "No, no—I won't take any cheek off of you, North. Don't you dare ask me if I've sworn off women and decided to try men."

Dexter shrugs innocently. "Hey, you've always had that big, unacknowledged crush on me, so I thought maybe..."

The men laugh like teenage boys at the dumb joke, and the waitress comes back to take their order.

"Two filets, medium rare," Dexter says, handing over their menus. "And thick-cut fries, please."

Theo drags his whiskey glass through the condensation on the table as he leans forward on one elbow. "So, yeah, the ladies have given me enough gray hairs for the time being." He hastily grabs a fistful of his artfully messy hair as proof, then lets go. "So I'm just doing the casual thing while I travel."

"As in one night stands?" Dexter tips his head at the bar, where two young women on stools are fighting hard not to get caught ogling Theo. It doesn't matter how many times it's happened, Dexter still marvels at the magnetic pull Theo's face and presence has on women he's never even spoken to.

Theo looks casually in the direction of the women, lifting his left eyebrow half an inch and dismissing the women with one twitch of his eye. "Yes," he says, "but no," he adds, glancing at the women again. "Too young. I've had my eye on sexy *mature* women of late. In fact, I recently had a fling with a woman of a certain age, and she quite nearly broke my heart." He puts one hand on his chest and winces for effect. "But that won't keep me from searching for the right one."

"The right older woman?" Dexter asks, his lips quirking as he tries not to smile. "Maybe all you need is to head home for a visit and some home-cooking from the original—and apparently the only—Mrs. Harris."

"Mum?" Theo laughs and throws an arm over the back of the booth while they wait for their steaks. "Yeah, I should visit her, to be honest. But work has kept me on the go. Serbia, Croatia, Puerto Rico, and I just arrived here in New York straight off a trip to Japan."

"We're going at this backwards, given that I asked for your work news first, but that's great, Theo. You're busy, you look well, and I read your latest piece—"

"The one that ran today about how the Japanese population is aging and putting the country in a perilous position economically?"

"Yes, the one about impending doom, a collapsing economy, and what sounds like our eventual future here in the States."

The waitress sets the steaks in front of the men, who order another round of drinks.

"Fabulous trip to Japan, that was," Theo says, cutting into his steak hungrily. "Depressing as all hell. Now tell me about your tangled web of work and women," he adds waving a fork around with one hand and his knife in the other. He resumes his cutting and puts the first bite of steak into his mouth.

Across the bar, the women who have been watching him openly

stare; they look on orgasmically as his lips move and he chews his meat. Dexter averts his gaze so that he doesn't laugh out loud.

"All of this is off the record and strictly between friends," Dexter says, lifting his own fork and knife and holding them gingerly. "The book is going well—you know I'm working on the one about Jack Hudson through the eyes of his First Lady—and we've covered a lot of ground."

"We're talking about that saucy little minx, are we? Ruby Hudson?" Theo's eyebrow shoots up past the half-inch mark this time and he looks like a fox in a henhouse. "A *very* sexy and more mature woman. And a widow, if memory serves..." he jokes, because of course the entire world knows Ruby's story. "Perhaps I could get her number?"

To his surprise, Dexter feels a bit territorial in the face of his old friend's teasing. "Ruby is amazing," he says, finally cutting a piece of steak. "And that's the problem, really."

Theo chews thoughtfully, realization dawning on his handsome face. "Ohhh, you fancy her, do you? You old goat!"

"I feel...conflicted," Dexter admits, choosing his words carefully. "She's smart and funny, and she's a very devoted mother. When I'm with her, or when we're having a Zoom call late at night, which is primarily how we work, I forget entirely that we're on a mission. I forget that I need to be professional and that I'm not a part of her story."

"But you want to be," Theo says, jabbing his knife in the air triumphantly. "I see you now, Dexter. Making a move on the former First Lady. Nice work, if you can get it."

"But I'm not," Dexter says, leaning across the table, dropping his voice, and glancing behind him over one shoulder to make sure no one is listening. "I'm *not* making a move on the former First Lady." The bar is playing jazz, and a saxophone solo rings out as Dexter searches for the right words. "I'm just finding that the more time I spend with her, the more I care about her. In a not very professional way. Which is..."

"Not very professional," Theo says dismissively, nodding. "Yeah, yeah—I get it. But sometimes the heart wants what it wants, right?"

"But the publishing house also wants what it wants, and what it *paid* me is a staggering advance for a book that I need to produce."

"And if you spend any more time with her you're not going to be able to resist, right? You're going to go crazy, like the madman you are, and rip your—"

"Hair out," Dexter says firmly. "Yes, I'm going to rip my hair out." He looks around again to see who might be close enough to hear. "But Theo, this isn't just any woman. Ruby is important; she's a *somebody*. Have you ever dated someone with their own Secret Service agent?"

For once, even Theo Harris looks cowed. He chews and swallows his bite of steak. "I have not."

"It's a bit intimidating."

"Quite," Theo agrees, eyes wide. "And do you even know if she feels the same?"

Dexter narrows his eyes, remembering their first dinner on Christmas Key, the day he took her to his tiny house on the island, and their time together in New York City. "I think she might," he finally says. "But she's—as you've said—mature, and therefore knows how to keep herself together. It's really best if I put just a little distance between us. At least for the time being."

Theo lifts his fresh glass of whiskey and makes a proposition. "I know you're on deadline with this book, though I assume you've got a bit of time to work with. So how about you let me introduce you to my editor. He's always looking for stringers to work on big stories, and frankly, you're a big enough name that your byline will be of value to him. Come with me to work on this piece about Russia and Ukraine."

"You want me to come to Russia?" Dexter sets his knife and fork on his plate with a clink.

"Well, technically Ukraine."

"Is that safe for journalists?"

"Dexter, old chap," Theo says, his eyes gleaming with mirth. "Apparently you aren't safe on a late-night Zoom call with a fifty-year-old blonde whose manners are impeccable and White House-worthy, so I can't imagine that Ukraine will be much more dangerous for you."

"You're probably right," Dexter says, lifting his whiskey glass in the air. "Salut!"

Theo clinks the edge of his own glass against Dexter's. "Salut, amigo. Now let's get you off of American soil for a bit, and away from your girl, shall we?"

Sunday

"It's a really good idea for someone living on an island to know boat basics," Linden says, holding out a rope for Sunday to take. "So go ahead and tie this just like I showed you, and then we'll untie it and redo it a few more times to make sure you've got it."

Linden is a fresh-faced high schooler with a mop of tawny auburn curls on top of his head, and braces that are embellished with bright blue rubber bands. Every inch of skin that's visible on the tall, lanky boy looks like it's been dipped in a box of freckles.

"Like this?" Sunday asks, holding up the rope to show him her knot. Ruby is on the bench next to her, tying her own knot, and the other two middle-aged people in Linden's class with them are a couple who frequent the bookstore and are always making requests for books that Ruby needs to order.

"Is it too early to have a grog when we're done with this?" Ruby says under her breath, muttering as she gets her knot tangled for the third time.

Sunday consults her watch. "It'll be noon by then, so I think as long as we order a basket of fries with our grog, we can call it lunch."

"Now," Linden says, pacing the boat from bow to stern and

admiring the work of his pupils, "if we take our ropes and undo the knots, I can show you how to tie up your boat. So let's do that."

"This feels like CPR training or something," Ruby says, breaking a sweat as she unties her knot. "But thanks for making me do it anyway. You never know when you might need to untie a boat, start the motor, and steal it to get away from the bad guys."

Sunday's eyes drift from the rope in her hands up to where Banks is standing on the dock, arms folded across his strong chest. He's wearing sunglasses, as usual, and scanning the area around the dock. All around them, boats rock lazily on the water, and from one of the vessels comes the unmistakable sound of two people "enjoying" their morning to the sounds of laid-back yacht rock.

"It's been a while since I've heard that sound," Ruby says, tipping her head in the direction of the boat. "Or since I made that sound."

Sunday coughs out a laugh that gets Linden's attention; his head jerks toward them like a teacher who's just realized that two of his pupils are gossiping instead of working.

"Sorry," Ruby mouths at him. She turns back to Sunday. "I see you eyeballing my main man over there," she says, letting her eyes flick in Banks's direction. "So maybe you're thinking of filling the evening air with the sounds of your own passion." She wiggles a shoulder suggestively, bumping it against Sunday as she does.

"Rubes," Sunday says, trying to frown and look serious. "We talked about this: Banks is here to work. Me messing with him could only end badly."

Ruby's eyes gleam with mischief. "Or it could end really, really good."

Sunday hides a laugh behind one hand, glancing at Banks again. Sure, it would be fun to have a little afternoon—or morning, or evening —delight with a man as handsome as Henry Banks. And it would take her mind off Peter and whatever shenanigans he's still up to in Washington. But she's just gotten her feet on the ground again after her trip to Tangier, and she's feeling better and more at peace than she has in a long time, with daily calls or texts to one or both of her daughters just to say hi, check in, or to share something funny that's happened. She's not prepared to throw all that away to be the island fling of a hot, smoldering, sexy, built-to-the-hilt Secret Service agent.

But still...she can't help looking. Banks shifts his weight as he turns his body to face the shoreline, and the muscles in his strong legs flex from under his khaki shorts. The sun has already turned him a burnished golden color in the months that they've been on Shipwreck Key, and his hair has lightened up a shade or two as well, glinting under the late morning sun as he scans the beach. Sunday bites her lower lip as she watches him.

"Hey," Ruby says, pulling Sunday back from her thoughts. "Want to come over for dinner tonight? I'm making grouper and the girls are doing all the side dishes."

Linden comes around again, talking loudly about knowing the parts of a boat, but Sunday tunes out all his talk of *fore* and *aft* and *bow* and *stern*. "Yeah," she says with a distracted smile. "I'd love to. Can I bring my homemade cheese biscuits?"

"Does our resident Secret Service agent have the abs of a man half his age?"

Sunday laughs. "Cheese biscuits it is."

* * *

The windows are all thrown wide open, and the sound of laughter comes from the kitchen as Sunday walks through the open front door and into Ruby's house at five-thirty that evening.

"Hello!" Sunday calls out, carrying her basket of cheese biscuits with both hands.

"In the kitchen, Sun!" Ruby shouts back.

Gathered around the marble island are Harlow and Athena, who are chopping vegetables and making a dill sauce, respectively, and Banks, who is sitting on a stool with a bottle of beer in one hand.

Sunday stops short. "Oh," she says, trying to snatch back the grin on her face before it disappears completely. She cranks up the wattage and smiles at all of them, letting her gaze rest on Banks. Normally she's not the least bit shy, but something about this man just makes her feel flustered and like a teenage girl with a crush. "Looks like security has gotten lax here on old Shipwreck Key," Sunday jokes, setting her basket on the counter. "Any crazy person could just walk in off the beach and into your house, Rubes."

Ruby is holding a spatula in one hand and she spins around to look at Sunday. "Well, any crazy person just did!"

Banks slides off the stool. "Ma'am, do you want me to go sit out front? I probably should."

Ruby turns on Banks now, letting the spatula flail around in the air. "No, no, no. We're having a family dinner here, and that includes you. Besides, you're about an inch from being dismissed from your post entirely, given the fact that Shipwreck Key is about the *least* dangerous place on the planet."

Banks looks concerned. "Ma'am, for your safety—"

Ruby cuts him off. "My safety isn't really in question. I feel very settled here," she says, walking around the kitchen as she opens and closes drawers, searching for something. The sound of the waves crashing on the beach comes in through the open windows, and through the kitchen doorway Sunday can see the long, gauzy dining room curtains billowing in on the ocean breeze. "I'm not afraid at all."

"Hey, Mom?" Athena says, licking a drip of dill sauce from the side of her hand as she mixes it in a bowl. "Do you think maybe part of the reason why you don't feel afraid is that Banks is so good at his job?"

"Ding, ding, ding," Sunday says, chiming in as she realizes that Ruby is threatening to send the most gorgeous man on the island back to D.C. "The man is good at his job, Rubes, so let him do it."

Ruby tips her head from side to side as she considers this. "I'm just feeling more and more like I'm getting to the point where I don't need a security detail. If I had somewhere to travel and I thought I needed it, I could definitely hire someone, but keeping Banks tied to this tiny island when he'd probably rather be free to go where he wants, live how he wants, and maybe find a date seems a little selfish, doesn't it?"

Sunday shoots daggers at Ruby with her eyes. *My god, what is she doing?!* Sunday thinks. *Trying to send my imaginary boyfriend back to Washington to find a date—does she want me to pounce on him? Beg him not to go? Wait...maybe I should.* She's eyeing Banks as he looks at Ruby, clearly trying to assess whether or not she's serious.

"Ma'am, I just want you to know that I'm extremely happy here," Banks says. He clears his throat. "There are far worse security details than this one, and you and I have been together for a long time. If I may say so myself, you won't find anyone to look after you the way I do."

Ruby's face softens. "Oh, Henry, I know that. You're the best at what you do, and I'm not really dismissing you. I'm just thinking ahead to the future. I still think letting the girls' security go was a wise choice. Having all three of you here was overkill, and Corbin and Eldrick are both young and really needed to be doing something more exciting."

Harlow pouts just enough that it's visible. Sunday knew from the things that Ruby had told her that Harlow had nursed a little crush on Eldrick, her own Secret Service agent, and that she'd occasionally said suggestive things about secretly dating him just to get the President's goat. When Ruby had ultimately decided that one agent on the island was enough, Harlow had been upset to see Eldrick—who'd been with her during the bar shooting she'd survived in New York—get on a boat to head back to Washington.

"Well, I'm not young, and living on the beach suits me just fine. No need for more excitement, more stress, or a bigger dating pool." His eyes skim the kitchen, snagging on Sunday so briefly that she isn't even sure that it happened. "In fact, I would argue that I probably have the best gig going of any agent I know, so if you would kindly keep it down about how much you don't need me anymore, then that would be great, thanks."

Everyone laughs at his unexpectedly sarcastic delivery.

"Hey," Ruby says, handing Sunday a tray with crackers and cheese spread. "Why don't you grab a drink from the fridge and you and Banks head outside. Enjoy the view for a couple of minutes while the girls and I finish up in here."

Sunday takes the crackers and blinks at Ruby like she's trying to send her a message in Morse code. "I could help you," she offers, stalling.

Ruby walks over to the fridge, pulls out a little individual can of Prosecco, pops the top, and thrusts it at Sunday. "Here, wine in a can. Go." She widens her eyes at Sunday and jerks her head at the porch.

Banks waits for Sunday to sit in one of the Adirondack chairs, then sinks into the one next to hers. She's set the plate of crackers on a low wooden table between them. He leans over and picks one up, dipping it in the wedge of soft cheese before taking a bite.

When the silence between them seems like it's gone on for a year, Banks finally speaks. "Does it make you nervous that I nearly saw you naked on the beach, ma'am?"

"Sunday," she reminds him. "And no—that was actually amusing. What makes me nervous is how much I want it to happen again." The words are out of her mouth before she even knows that they're climbing up her throat. Sunday puts a hand to her lips in horror. "Oh my god."

Banks gives an uncharacteristic laugh, and it's so loud that Sunday turns to him in surprise.

"That was maybe the last thing I expected you to say," Banks admits, shaking his head in wonder. He gives the ocean a long, hard stare before speaking again. "But I'm not going to lie to you, Sunday, it's crossed my mind a time or two."

Sunday's face flames and she lifts the cold can of Prosecco to her lips, drinking the bubbly liquid like it's a Diet Coke, but then remembering it isn't soda when her head instantly starts to buzz. She follows his lead and looks out at the water. "You're on Ruby's detail," she says softly. "We probably shouldn't even be flirting."

"We're two consenting adults, and I'm not *your* security, so I don't think you need to worry about us crossing any lines. Besides, we're just talking."

As Banks sips his beer she notices that the bottle looks small in his large hand. Even his arm dwarfs things. Banks is made of muscle, and every inch of skin that Sunday can see makes her want to take a long drink of him like she just took from her can of wine.

"It's still complicated, and you know it is," she says, but in a mild tone. Even to her own ear, Sunday sounds like a woman who isn't entirely convinced by the words coming out of her mouth.

"From what you told me the other day on the beach, you're single—and well on your way to a divorce. I've been divorced for seven years. That's pretty uncomplicated."

Sunday looks over her shoulder at the window that's open between the porch and the dining room; she doesn't want Harlow and Athena to hear her propositioning a man who they see as a professional person on their mother's staff.

"Do you want to come over later?" she asks in a near whisper. "For a *walk*," Sunday adds. "Just a walk to look at the moon."

Banks takes a long minute to answer. "I could take a walk."

They're sitting together, contemplating this so-called walk and whether it's possibly a euphemism for anything more, when the girls walk out to the picnic table at the other end of the porch, which has been set with an orange linen tablecloth, brown napkins encircled by cut topaz napkin rings, and plates that Sunday knows belonged to Ruby's mother. She jumps up from the chair, still holding her can of wine, which now looks tacky next to the Pinterest-worthy table.

"Let me take that, Aunt Sun," Harlow says, sweeping by and taking the Prosecco can from her. She hands her a bottle of wine instead. "If you could just set this on the table, that would be great."

"Shall we?" Banks holds out a hand in the direction of the table, indicating that he'll follow her lead.

Athena is leaning over three hurricane lamps, lighting candles with a long-handled lighter, so Sunday takes a seat on the bench with her back to the water, eyeing Banks to see which spot he'll choose.

Out of habit, he sits facing the water, with his back to the house, which is better for him when it comes to observing. It's true that things have gotten far more lax as the months have gone on, but the man is a Secret Service agent, and there's no way he'll stop taking the simple precautions that have been drilled into him so deeply that he'll probably always take them, even when his years of guarding and protecting are long behind him.

"So, Aunt Sunday," Athena says, sitting next to Banks on the bench. "I hear you and Mom are going to enter a sailing race."

Sunday's laugh bubbles over and she's immediately at ease again. The obvious heat between her and Banks is easily smoothed over by the chatter of Ruby's girls, and once Harlow is seated next to Sunday, they start in right away with teasing and ribbing one another, and it keeps Ruby, Sunday, and Banks in stitches.

By the time the sun has set completely and the only light on the porch is coming from the candles on the table, they've finished a bottle and a half of wine, all the grouper, the grilled asparagus, and Harlow is going for a third helping of whipped sweet potatoes with butter.

"Girl. All you've done on Shipwreck Key is eat," Athena says, teasing her sister.

Harlow shrugs. "Well, I barely ate in New York because I was too busy working and going out in the evening with my coworkers, so I'm making up for it now. Besides, guys like thick girls. Right, Banks?"

Banks holds up both hands in surrender, looking at his plate. "I don't like to comment on the appearance of ladies, nor can I speak for all men," he says diplomatically, dropping his napkin on the table.

Ruby laughs over her glass of wine. "Banks is a professional when it comes to riding the fence. I admire that. Very tactful." She bows her head at him.

This evening has been a total departure for Banks. For as long as he's been with the family, Sunday knows that he's always kept a respectful distance, so she can only imagine that Ruby pressed him pretty hard when it came to joining them for dinner tonight.

"Can I help you clean up, Rubes?" Sunday offers, gathering her plate and silverware as she stands up.

"No, absolutely not," Ruby says sternly, waving a hand at Sunday. "You just relax. The girls and I are doing everything."

"Actually, if you don't mind, I think I'll call it a night then," Sunday says, carrying her plate into the kitchen anyway. "I'm pretty tired," she calls back over her shoulder, hoping that leaving just after seven o'clock doesn't seem too abrupt.

"You know what?" Ruby says loudly. "I'm giving Banks the evening off, but only if he'll agree to walk you home."

Sunday walks back outside to give Ruby and the girls hugs, and to thank them for dinner. "I drove my golf cart, but thanks anyway," she says.

"You also drank a fair amount before and during dinner, so I don't want you to drive. If Banks walks you along the beach, you'll be there in ten minutes."

"She's right," Banks says, rising and picking up his own plate. "I'm happy to walk you."

It's in Sunday's nature to protest, but then she realizes that she'll be working against her own interest if she does.

"Okay," she relents. "That would be nice. I can just come back tomorrow for my cart."

"Leave everything," Ruby says, looking pleased. Harlow reaches over and takes Banks's plate from his hands. "You two have a nice walk."

Just as he had when he held out a hand for Sunday to take her seat at the table first, he holds out a hand for her to lead the way down the stairs and onto the sand. As they walk away from Ruby's house, Sunday glances back at the candles flickering on the porch, and at the lights that shine brightly from inside the kitchen. There's a warmth to Ruby and to her life that makes Sunday feel like a moth to a flame, and there have been moments during their friendship when she's felt that she, Sunday Bellows Bond, is nothing but a rootless young girl searching for something to anchor her. But for Ruby, it seems to come so easily, in spite of the fact that she lost her father at such a young age. Everyone around her feels her calm, weighted presence, and this is something that Sunday has always loved about Ruby.

"Penny for your thoughts," Banks says, walking along beside her at a leisurely pace. Ruby's house fades into the distance behind them. The sun has set completely, and the moon is lighting their way.

Sunday stops to kick off her sandals so that she can carry them in her hand instead. "You know," she says, standing upright again. "I was actually thinking about my friendship with Ruby."

Banks nods as they start walking together again. His hands are in the pockets of his knee-length cargo shorts. "I've enjoyed watching you two together over the years."

This surprises Sunday, though it shouldn't. In her mind, Secret Service agents are always there, but they fade into the background. She's not sure why she imagines that they tune out most of the personal conversation that goes on around them, but of course they wouldn't. It's only human nature to listen and observe, not to mention being the most important part of an agent's job.

"I don't think I could have survived in Washington without her."

"Is that why you wanted to come down here? If you don't mind me asking, of course."

Sunday thinks about this. She shifts her sandals to the hand furthest from Banks, and then her free hand brushes against his accidentally, sending a shiver of pleasure up her arm. "I wouldn't say I came here because I don't think that I could survive without her, no..."

"I didn't really mean it like that," Banks clarifies. "I guess more like, do you think you came down here because you two have become one another's support systems, and maybe you feel like her getting settled on an unfamiliar island would be easier with her best friend by her side?"

Sunday frowns. "Could be. And now that you mention it, maybe my going through a divorce is a time when I feel, once again, like I need Ruby to lean on. But I never think of it that way," she says firmly, turning to look up at him. "And I would never come here and intentionally be a burden on Ruby. Never." Panic rises in Sunday's chest at the thought of moving to Shipwreck Key and inadvertently cramping Ruby's style with her neediness.

"Whoa," Banks says, holding up a hand. "Stand down, soldier. I would never think for a minute that you were a burden on Ruby, nor would she think that. I can guarantee it. From where I stand, she's been infinitely happier here on the island since you and Harlow and Athena all joined her."

Sunday releases a breath. "You're right. She's not like that. But I never asked her what she thought about me coming here, I just told her I was doing it."

Banks chuckles. "That's alright. It's a free country and you're a woman who can move about and do what she wants without permission."

"Finally," Sunday says quietly.

They walk in amiable silence for several paces.

"How does that feel?" Banks asks her, eyes looking ahead at the dark beach that unspools before them. "To finally be free?"

The sand is cool and damp under Sunday's bare feet and she takes a second to feel it and appreciate it. "Well," she finally says, her knuckles brushing against Banks's again. "I guess first you'd have to know what it's like to *not* be free."

"Mmm," Banks says noncommittally, which encourages Sunday to continue.

"I married Peter at twenty-two, and when I did, I had no idea that we were...incompatible, as it were."

Banks clears his throat. "Ma'am, it's well known that Mr. Bond dances at the other end of the ballroom, if you don't mind me saying so."

Sunday bursts out in a loud, hearty laugh. "Oh, I must be getting old, Henry. That's a new one." Without warning, her laughter turns into unexpected tears.

"Sunday," Banks says, reaching for her hand as he stops walking. "Hey, I'm sorry. I didn't mean to upset you."

Sunday closes her eyes and shakes her head. She's mortified. "God, Henry. It's not you—please, don't worry about it." She sniffles and wipes her eyes with the back of her hand. "I've buried my feelings about my marriage pretty deep inside of me, and I think that every so often I just reach in there and hit a nerve or something. You know?" She sniffles again. "I know most of what Peter's done, and what I don't know I'm fine never hearing about. But there's a little part of me that feels—I don't know, humiliated? Yeah, humiliated. I feel ashamed when I realize that *everyone* knew what he was up to."

"Well, not everyone," Banks says in a reassuring tone. "I'm pretty sure my mom doesn't know."

This makes Sunday laugh again, and she's grateful for the joke to lighten the mood. "On top of that, there's the failure of going through a divorce."

"Which I do understand," Banks adds, still holding her hand in his warm one. He absentmindedly strokes the soft skin on the top of her hand with his thumb. "I felt like a huge failure when Denise and I split up. She got the house, the dog, and the car that was paid for, and I got to slink away with my tail between my legs."

Sunday is watching him now, and he doesn't shy away from the topic, which she admires. "Can I ask what wrong?"

"You can ask, but I'm not sure I can even tell you. Actually," he says, reconsidering. "I can. Denise never fully appreciated how much of your life you have to devote to the Secret Service. At various times she accused me of being in love with Ruby, which I'm not," he clarifies quickly, "nor was I ever. And she also said ridiculous things about how I needed to get a life of my own because I was too tangled up in the First Family's."

"But that's your job!" Sunday protests.

"It is. But in Denise's defense—much as I hate to defend her—my job left little time for a personal life. She wanted kids, but it always felt like the wrong time to me, and it also felt a little irresponsible. It's hard to have a pregnant wife waiting for you at home while you're flinging yourself between the President and someone who wants to do him harm. All I could think of was leaving her a widow with a baby to care for, and I...I just couldn't." He squeezes Sunday's hand and then lets it go, putting both of his hands on top of his head as he turns to look out at the water. "She was right to leave me. She was."

Sunday says nothing, but she puts a hand on his strong back to let him know that she's there and that she hears him.

Banks lets his hands fall to his sides, but he doesn't turn to look at Sunday just yet. "She's married now to a guy who works in D.C. but comes home to the suburbs every night to have dinner with her. They've got two little boys and she still has our old dog. She's on the PTA at the kids' school, and they take skiing trips every winter as a family. I could have never given her all of that."

Sunday frowns. "You two keep in touch?" The idea of her keeping in touch with Peter is a foreign one; their girls are grown, and there's no need.

When Banks gives a hard laugh, Ruby can feel it through the hand that's still on his back. "No. We don't. But I know enough people who know how to find out information on pretty much any topic you could imagine, so...it's not hard to find out what she's up to." He grows quiet. "I just wanted to know that she was fine. I'm not hung up on her or anything. It's been seven years, and honestly, I'm happy for her."

Sunday smiles as she stands behind him. She can tell that he is, in fact, over his ex-wife, but that there's a part of him that cares about her, and that he truly just wanted to make sure she was okay.

"There are things we never fully let go of," Sunday says, "and it's okay if love is one of them. Can I tell you a story?"

Banks turns to look at her, face open and curious. "Of course. Let's walk. I want to hear it."

As they start to walk again, Sunday tells Banks about getting pregnant at seventeen. She tells him the same things she told her girls about the nuns who ran the home, about finding an apartment after giving Benjamin up for adoption, and about getting her two-year degree before meeting Peter. When she's done, they're standing on the sand in front of her house, right where Banks caught her floating in the water naked that day after she'd had the infuriating phone call with Peter.

Banks doesn't say anything for a long moment, but then he reaches out and takes Sunday's hand. "You're an incredible woman," he says, looking into her eyes. The moonlight reflects off the water just feet from where they stand. "I'd ask to kiss you, but I feel like it's best if this is just a walk home--at least for tonight."

Sunday takes a step back from him, letting his hand fall away from hers.

He's not wrong. She has things she needs to do and closure she needs to find before she opens her heart to someone else, but she can't lie to herself about the fact that she *wants* him to kiss her.

"Thanks for the walk, Henry," she says, dipping her chin shyly and looking up at him through the hair that blows across her face in the light breeze.

With a last look back at him over her shoulder, Sunday crosses the sand with her shoes in one hand, walks up the stairs, and lets herself into her dark house through the door that leads into the kitchen. She doesn't turn on the lights, but instead stands at her kitchen sink and watches as Banks turns and starts the walk back to Ruby's house.

Peter

~∂↝⌒

"Peter Bond, former Vice President," Peter says as he leans into the mirror in the hotel bathroom, straightening the tie around his neck. "Pleasure to meet you—Peter Bond, former V.P.," he says, this time winking at his reflection.

He's just spent the night at a hotel in downtown Miami, and when he walks back out into the bedroom, he knows he'll find a hungover male model who's half his age spread out enticingly on the king-sized bed. Peter has a system for finding companionship in every city he goes to, and it never fails: he sends his assistant out to search for the best-looking guy hanging around the hotel bar, one who is clearly waiting for an older man to approach him. Edgar, Peter's assistant, sighs and shakes his head every time, but he knows what to look for and so he does it, sending the catch of the day up the elevator with strict instructions to keep his cell phone off and to be prepared to be discreet.

"Good morning," the male model says as Peter emerges from the bathroom in a bespoke navy blue suit, blue-and-white pinstriped shirt, and red tie. "You're looking like breakfast in that tie," he says, wrapping the sheet around his narrow waist and sitting up on his knees on the bed with a sexy grin.

How is it that people in their twenties wake up looking like this? Peter

149

thinks, stopping in his tracks to watch this toned, tanned, completely chiseled man go from asleep to fully awake in the blink of an eye. At nearly sixty, it takes Peter an hour, three cups of coffee, and two newspapers before he even feels like speaking to another human.

"Good morning," Peter says with a crisp nod. He's forgotten the boy's name already--not that it matters much. Wordlessly, Peter pulls his wallet from inside his jacket pocket and slides out a few hundred dollar bills. He tosses them on the messy bedding.

The man-boy in his bed looks at the money, appearing crestfallen. "I don't...you don't need to...I'm not—"

"It's fine," Peter says, waving the money away. "I'm not calling you a prostitute or anything—"

"Sex worker," the young man says, looking at Peter like he's teaching him something important. "We refer to them as sex workers now, and there's no stigma attached. I'm just saying that I'm not one."

Peter holds up a hand like a stop sign. "Regardless. I've been young and hungry, and I could have used a few bucks every once in a while."

"But, I—"

"I'm late for a meeting," Peter says brusquely, reaching for the handle of his suitcase. He starts to roll it to the door, but then turns back to the naked man in his bed. "Feel free to get room service if you like. Check-out is at eleven."

The door closes behind him and Peter rolls his suitcase to the elevator. He heads down to the lobby, where he's meeting his campaign advisors.

On the ride to the Mayor's office, Delia and Umberto, who Peter has hand-picked to help guide him as he prepares to run for President in the next election, consult their phones, each other, and talk around Peter non-stop as they plan his day and make decisions about meals, detours, and meetings. But Peter is distracted, thinking of the stranger he's just left in his hotel room.Why has it never bothered him to share the kind of intimacies with strange men that he couldn't even bring himself to share with his wife? It's been years since Sunday has seen Peter walking around in boxer shorts or simply brushing his teeth. Their lives have become so separate that there's almost no overlap between them, and somehow they've both accepted this.

"Peter?" Delia is saying his name and looking at him expectantly. By the look on Umberto's face, it's clear that Delia has been talking to Peter as he watches Miami drift by outside the car window. "Are you good with that?"

"Hmm? Sorry," Peter says, clearing his throat and tugging at his necktie, which has suddenly started to strangle him. "I was thinking of something else."

"We have the ten o'clock meeting with the lawyers, and then after that, there's a luncheon at a steakhouse in Key Biscayne that you're scheduled to attend. You're not speaking at that one, but at three o'clock, we have you slated as a speaker at the teachers' union meeting in North Miami."

Peter takes a deep breath, filling his lungs. "Yes, that all sounds fine," he says, nodding. Actually, meeting with the lawyers isn't at the top of the list of things he wants to do, but he'll do it because he has to. And because Sunday is demanding it.

Seeing her makes him nervous, to be honest. The limo driver pulls up to a tall building in downtown Miami and Peter throws open the door and steps out. He's not one for taking a moment to prepare himself mentally for things--quite the opposite, in fact; Peter much prefers to go straight into battle, guns blazing, without giving himself time to second guess anything.

He stands on the sidewalk, looking at the buildings around him. They're sleek, curved, made entirely of glass, and with just a hint of the Art Deco style that Miami and South Beach are known for. Behind him--if he were to turn around and look--he would see a gigantic billboard hovering over the street advertising the latest in Calvin Klein men's underwear. And the billboard wouldn't simply be of interest to Peter because there's a gorgeous man clad in nothing but a small patch of tight, white cotton, but because the man wearing that white cotton is the very same young, handsome man that Peter left in his hotel room not an hour before.

But so focused is he on his showdown with Sunday that he doesn't even clock the advertisement, and therefore has no clue that he spent the night before with a supermodel, and not with some random guy from a bar who needs his three hundred dollars in cash.

"We're on the twenty-first floor," Delia says, leading the way with her phone in hand. She walks confidently into the lobby of the building, her heels click-clacking against the marble floors.

Inside the designated meeting room on the twenty-first floor is a long table filled with both legal teams. Peter enters the room sandwiched between Delia and Umberto, and he chooses a seat at the end of the table, as far away from Sunday as he can possibly get.

At her end, Sunday sits calmly, looking tanned and confident. She has her hands folded on the table, and her hair has gotten longer and lighter from living full-time in the sun. Peter eyes her carefully, shrewdly taking note of each and every change. She's no longer wearing her wedding ring, and on each hand she wears a heavy stone on a gold band instead. Around her neck is a thick gold necklace with a tag on it that clearly marks it as Tiffany's. Sunday looks more relaxed than Peter ever remembers seeing her. She's dressed in a loose, flowing pink dress, just a touch of makeup, and a smile.

She looks at ease, and he doesn't like it.

"If we could get started here," Peter's head attorney says, calling the meeting to order.

Sunday lifts a glass of still water and sips it calmly.

"We'd like to begin with our first request, which is for non-disclosure," Sunday's attorney, a woman named Glenda Fine, says as she consults the file in front of her. "Mr. Bond will respect Mrs. Bond's request for privacy on all matters pertaining to their marriage and to her life prior to their marriage. He will not speak of her publicly unless it's to sing her praises as a mother, and as a former Second Lady."

Peter laughs out loud. "She can't do that," he says, tapping the polished mahogany table with one finger repeatedly. "It's not her place to muzzle me. If anything, I should be requesting that *she* keep her mouth shut about anything pertaining to our marriage or its dissolution. I have very good reasons for speaking up about the things that happened between me and Sunday, and I would venture to say that she does not."

"Peter," Sunday says, blinking slowly and looking bored of this discussion already, though he knows her well enough to know that she's putting on a show for everyone in the room; she's as nervous as a long-tailed cat in a room full of rocking chairs. "My life is my business. I do not exist solely to make you look good and then to let you wipe your feet on my back when you get tired of using me as the perfect wife and mother."

"I think *perfect* is a big stretch," Peter says, sitting back in his chair. He's amused to watch her negotiate with him in front of all these high-powered attorneys. Sunday, a woman with a two-year college degree, trying to talk her way out of a corner in a room filled with lawyers, college-educated advisors, and Peter, the former Vice President of the United States. It's almost laughable. "I might mention here that the issue at hand is a thorny one, given that you sent your only biological child away to be raised by strangers."

Every single person in the room finds something to look at or to occupy them as the tension between Peter and Sunday ratchets up several notches. Delia picks up her phone and scrolls through emails, and all of Sunday's attorneys consult the files on the table.

Outside the window, twenty-one floors below, carefully planted palm trees wave on the street under the late October sun, and women walk around bare-legged, soaking up the warmth and catching the admiring gazes of men in business suits. Restaurants serve brunch at outdoor bistro tables to a mixed crowd of models, office-dwellers, and international travelers, everyone documenting their picturesque morning on social media, via FaceTime, or in photos of their Cuban coffees, mimosas decorated with flowers, and fluffy pastry filled with whipped salmon or artisanal jam.

But inside this building the rooms are frosty, kept chilled to sixty-eight degrees year-round, and the lighting is stark, diffused only by the sunlight filtering in through the windows. Peter wonders if anything happy ever goes on at this particular board room table, but ultimately he doesn't care, so long as he walks out of here and out onto the street with another win under his belt.

"Peter," Sunday says, pushing back from the table slightly and then standing. She walks over to the windows and looks at the street scene far below. "I took the girls to Tangier Island recently. We stayed there, and went to Minnie's house. I took them to meet my high school boyfriend's mother, and while we were there, they had the chance to hear the entire

story--all of it. Nothing you could tell them would shock them now."
She turns and faces him, the faraway look in her eyes as she'd gazed at the
cars and people below now replaced by a fiery determination. "So you go
ahead and say what you need to say about me. I want you to. I hope it
works out in your favor to turn me into a villain--I really do."

Sunday's legal team visibly deflates, but no one stops her from
speaking.

"I don't care what the rest of America thinks of me anymore,"
Sunday says, walking down the length of the table so that she's standing
just three feet away from him, forcing him to look up at her like a little
boy being scolded by his mother. He tries to retain his composure, but
it's nearly impossible given her stance. "The two most important people
in my life know the truth now, so you telling everyone else that I got
pregnant too young and chose to give my baby to a loving family won't
make me look bad. Me leaving a small town and trying to make something of my life won't make me look bad. And me leaving you when
everyone--and I mean *everyone*--knows what you've been doing behind
my back for the entire length of our marriage won't reflect poorly on
me. So you think about that before you sit down with Diane Sawyer and
try to drag me through the mud."

"There are optics to this thing, Sunday, and how I look is important
if I'm going to make a run for the Oval Office--"

"Listen," Sunday says, shaking her head. "Not that you're asking me
to, but I've forgiven you. I truly have." Her face and her voice soften
considerably as she looks down at the man who she'd clung to for
decades--out of hope, out of security, out of a sense of duty, and sometimes even out of love--and she reaches out with one hand as if she
might touch his face, but then pulls her hand back before she actually
does. She looks terrifyingly calm. "But maybe you need to think about
this as an opportunity to be your true self. Maybe you should consider
coming out publicly. You have no idea how impactful that could be."

Peter wants to shove back from the table, to shut her up, to make
her stop talking this way in front of all these people. He's a sixty-year-old
man! He's a famous politician! There's no way he can just be gay and
live his life. There's no way people will vote for someone who they see as
living an alternative lifestyle...or is there? Instead of stopping her, Peter's

eyes linger on the face of his wife. She's no longer the young, fearful girl he married when she was twenty-two and he was twenty-eight. They've been through it all, way too much to be as innocent and unworldly as they once were. And while Sunday is angry and she no longer loves him (this he knows with full certainty), perhaps there's a part of her that wishes him well. This would be just like Sunday to put her own feelings aside in order to give him loving advice, and it stuns him that she could still be capable of kindness towards him after all he's put her through.

"Think about it," Sunday says, finally reaching out with her hand and resting it on his shoulder. He doesn't flinch or look away. "And trust me, Peter, the truth can set you free."

With one final long, meaningful look, Sunday turns around and walks back to her seat at the other end of the table, her long, pink dress floating behind her. She sits, folds her hands again, and stares at Peter placidly.

"Okay," Peter's lead attorney says, passing a piece of paper across the table to Glenda Fine. Everyone behaves as if they haven't just listened to Sunday tell the former Vice President to come out of the closet and run for President as an openly gay man. "With that, I think we're prepared to negotiate the terms of this divorce. Here's what we're prepared to offer."

An hour later, Peter and Sunday exit the building from different sides--Sunday out the back and into a waiting Mercedes, and Peter out the front and into his limousine--with their signatures on the document. As far as Peter is concerned, his marriage is completely behind him, but he knows that the battle to make himself look presidential in the eyes of the public is all ahead of him. And he'll do whatever he has to do to make that happen.

The door to his limo shuts behind him and the sleek car pulls out into traffic, the reflection of the giant Calvin Klein billboard reflected on the shiny black hood of the car.

Ruby

The book club meets two weeks before Thanksgiving, and in honor of the season, they've decided the theme is anything *but* turkey and pie. Marigold has arrived with her famous chicken fried rice and dumplings, Heather has baked almond toffee bars and brought a tub of vanilla ice cream, Ruby's carefully layered basil, tomatoes, and thick, fresh slices of mozzarella on a plate and drizzled the whole thing with oil and vinegar, and Sunday shows up with mini hotdogs in tiny little buns, with a spicy mustard and a tangy ketchup to dip them in.

"This is a total hodgepodge," Ruby laughs, looking at the table. Her only concession to the holiday that's on the horizon has been to cover the table with a yellow cloth covered in hand-embroidered fall leaves (a gift from the wife of the former Governor of Maine), and to hang paper leaves on all her windows so that passerby can see that she's decorated for fall.

"It looks delicious," Molly says, walking in with a bottle of vodka in one hand and a bottle of cranberry juice in the other. She's also holding a clear bag with three limes in it. "I brought the makings for Cape Cods," she says, holding up the items.

"Cranberries feel *very* Thanksgiving-y to me," Marigold says, lifting an eyebrow. "But I'm gonna overlook it, since I'm ready for a Cape Cod."

Ruby smiles at the women--her friends--as they file in and start the usual routine of hugs, chitchat, and filling plates with appetizers. It's good to hear their voices in her bookshop, and the warmth that each woman exudes is almost tangible.

At the front of the store, Vanessa chooses a Christmas jazz playlist and gets the sound just right.

"Heyyyy!" Marigold calls out, turning to look through the three rooms of the bookshop to where Vanessa is still standing behind the front desk. "This is *definitely* holiday music! We're doing an anti-holiday themed book club meeting!"

"What are you, the holiday police?" Molly asks with a frown. "Simmer down, sweet cheeks, and let the girl play what she wants."

Heather sits in the chair next to Molly's, elbowing her playfully. "Never would have pegged you for a Christmas music fan."

"I'm one of those broads who looks tough on the outside, but on the inside I'm a big marshmallow," Molly says, knocking back a swig of her vodka-heavy Cape Cod. She winks at Heather. "But don't spread that around."

Ruby is as charmed by the women as she always is, but her mind is partially elsewhere as she scoops fried rice onto her appetizer plate and adds an almond toffee bar, a scoop of ice cream, a few dumplings, some caprese salad, and a miniature hot dog with condiments. She'll surely pay for it later as she lies awake half the night wondering what in the hell she ate at book club, but it'll be worth it for the fun of a true junk food fest with the girls.

"Where are Harlow and Athena?" Molly asks as she pops a tiny hot dog into her mouth.

"They went to D.C. together to pack up Athena's apartment," Ruby says from where she's standing at the table. "They've both officially decided to give up their apartments up north and stay down here a bit longer, but because of the wonder of the internet, they can work remotely, which is incredible. Wasn't like that when we were young, was it ladies?"

"Not even," Sunday agrees. "But good for them. I love that they're staying, and frankly, I'm a little jealous. A part of me wishes my girls were in a position to move down here and live on Shipwreck."

"But you've made your peace with them, and they're both doing good things, so that's what matters," Molly says, lifting her Cape Cod in a toast. She takes a sip.

"I'm eternally grateful for that," Sunday says, crossing her legs and balancing her overly full plate perilously on one knee. "And I've even found some peace with Peter, which is nothing short of a miracle."

The women grow silent. Peter isn't a frequent topic of conversation, and Sunday hasn't said much to them at all about her impending divorce.

"I went up to Miami a few weeks ago and met with Peter and all the lawyers," she says, holding her drink. "We had some words, and I told him that I don't care anymore what he says about me. I mean it, too."

"Good for you," Molly says. "Holding onto that bitterness will eat you up from the inside, like swallowing battery acid."

"That's the truth," Marigold says around a swig of her drink. "Take it from someone who's been divorced long enough to have an opinion on bitterness, forgiveness, and moving on."

"We don't talk much about you and Cobb," Heather says, glancing at Marigold from across the circle that they've made of their chairs.

"That's intentional," Marigold admits. "Cobb and I have a lot of stuff. We have a complicated past, and, to be perfectly honest, things are still a bit muddy. But that's a story for another time. I want to hear more about Peter."

"That's all there is, really," Sunday says, looking at the paper leaves on the window. The sky outside has darkened, and the Christmas music, while it doesn't go with the food, still makes everything feel cozy. "Well, that and I told him it was time to come out of the closet and face the world as the gay man that he is."

Molly chokes and sends vodka and cranberry juice flying as she tries to clear her windpipe. "He's gay?" she chokes out, covering her mouth with the back of her hand.

Marigold laughs. "As a picnic basket. You didn't know that?"

Sunday looks at Marigold. "Is it that obvious?"

Marigold shrugs. "I've known a lot of gay men, and I think there are some tells, yeah. Also there are rumors," she says apologetically. "Sorry, but word gets around."

"Maybe in the world that you all inhabit," Molly says, still clearing her throat. "But I don't indulge in idle gossip or read the kinds of trashy magazines that talk about things like this." She looks around disapprovingly. "Still, if the man is gay, he's gay, and good for you that you told him to just come out with it. I don't support people living lives that aren't authentically their own, and I think it's high time we let people come out of their damn closets and live however they want."

"Well said," Ruby agrees. "I know he has to contend with other things like how his personal life appears to voters, and that he has to consider how everything he does looks to the public, but living a life that's defined by secrets can't feel good." She pauses. "If I could, I'd ask my own husband how that felt to be in love with someone else and to have a child that he had to hide away from the world."

"It's not quite the same thing though, is it?" Molly asks, looking back and forth between the two women. "If the President had come forward and told the world that he had two families, I don't think voters would have taken too kindly to that. But if a man running for office simply wants to be himself, then I think more people will accept it."

"You'd be surprised," Ruby says, feeling the weight of the public's sentiment--something she knows firsthand. "People can be *very* judgmental about...well, everything."

"What's the worst thing you ever got from the media?" Marigold asks Ruby.

"Um...I think the worst thing I ever experienced was how hard they were on my girls." She feels her heart constrict at the memory of how difficult Athena in particular had it, with the way the media portrayed her every gawky, awkward move as a young teenager, passive-aggressively poking fun at the way she wore her hair, how she looked with braces, and even the way she smiled. They'd also been hard on Harlow, discussing ad nauseam her every misstep and showcasing her most outrageous outfits as if she were a grown woman who had made some sort of agreement to be in the public eye, which she most certainly was not and had not.

"But for me, personally," Ruby continues, "I think that my worst experience was the way they made me look and feel after Jack died. Every photo I saw of myself made me look like a crazed, traumatized widow."

"And you weren't?" Molly asks, though not unkindly.

"I was shocked, I think," Ruby admits. "And maybe traumatized by the amount of scrutiny I was under, but I was not crazed or traumatized by his death itself and the other events that it uncovered. I already had some hint that Jack had fathered a child with another woman because of the DNA test that Harlow had taken, so that was all shocking but not mind-blowing." She sets her plate on her lap and holds her drink in one hand. "I just felt like everywhere I went, they were waiting for me to break down or do something that would make me look insane. And in turn, it kind of drove me insane. I felt paranoid all the time. I started to believe people were going through my trash looking for things to write about me."

"They probably were." Marigold nods. "In Hollywood the paparazzi are well known for digging through trash cans."

"Yeah, I don't trust the media in general, but I understand that they serve a purpose. So I get Peter's hesitancy to come out, although I also get how much his lifestyle has hurt Sunday." Ruby looks at her friend with love and sympathy, and Sunday smiles back. "Coming out will be hard for him to do, but I think you got the closure you needed with him, didn't you, Sun?"

Sunday nods slowly. "I do. For now. In a really small amount of time this year I've moved incredibly far and fast towards healing. I moved here, I left Washington behind, I went home to Tangier Island, I got my girls to understand me better, and I said what I needed to say to Peter. I'm feeling really good."

"Plus you got that beefcake always checking you out," Molly says, nodding in Banks's direction. Whereas he'd started out standing at the side of the room at full attention every time he was in the bookstore, Banks has begun to sit in a chair more casually, one leg crossed over the other as he pages through a book from the shelves. He's looking and feeling less like a professional Secret Service agent constantly assessing the danger of a situation, and more like a bodyguard who happens to be close by in case he's needed.

"Shhh!" Sunday says, motioning with her hand for Molly to keep it down. "He's not checking me out."

Molly lifts one eyebrow like she wants to argue this, but instead she uses her plastic fork to spear a bite of mozzarella and tomato, bringing it to her mouth and popping it in.

As usual, the group hasn't even mentioned the book they've been reading these past couple of weeks, but Ruby doesn't fret about that one bit. This ability to talk to the other women about the things that come up in their lives is so much more valuable than discussing any book they might choose to read.

And there's more that Ruby would share, but instead she munches thoughtfully on the dumplings as she listens to the women talk about Bev Byer and the way he's been acting grumpy lately every time any of them set foot inside The Frog's Grog.

"Exactly!" Heather says. "I was in there the other day and he was all bent out of shape about the way people were drinking down at the Black Pearl with their dinner every night, but not stopping in at The Frog's Grog lately for a nightcap. He said something about The Black Pearl stealing his grog recipe and advertising it on their website so that visitors to the island went straight to the restaurant."

"Well, they're missing out then," Molly says. "The Frog's Grog is a Shipwreck Key staple. If you come here and you don't stop by for one of Bev's grogs, then can you really say you've been to Shipwreck?"

The conversation goes on like this as Ruby nods and smiles, but she's lost in thought remembering the emails she'd just gotten that afternoon. First was a follow-up from her attorney regarding the message she'd received from Etienne while she was in New York. She still hasn't addressed Etienne directly, though the email has been on her mind almost daily. She isn't sure how she's supposed to feel about Jack's death leaving Etienne and her son high and dry, but she knows how she *does* feel, which is conflicted. On the one hand, she should be angry and shouldn't care at all about what happens to her late husband's mistress or the child he fathered with her. On the other, she knows that by sharing the news of Jack's suicide with the world, she essentially cut off Etienne's ability to access the insurance policy that Jack had intended for her to have. And she feels guilty about that because she intercepted something that was Jack's intention. So it's complicated--there's no easy way to look at it, and there's no one size fits all kind of answer for the situation. Her attorney has been looking into ways to address the insurance company on Etienne's behalf, which Ruby feels in her heart will alleviate some of her own guilt, but paying out of pocket to have someone look into the matter kind of grinds her gears. It's a constant push-pull of emotions.

The other email she received was from Dexter, who has been weirdly quiet since she left New York. They've been in touch a few times and he's repeatedly insisted that rather than doing any Zoom calls for the time being, he'd like to work with the material he has and see where that puts him. This new email today was short and to the point, and as she'd sat at her computer in the tiny upstairs office over the bookshop, she'd felt her cheeks bloom red just reading it:

Ruby--

I'm going to be on a tiny hiatus from working on the book. I think it's best. A little perspective always helps when trying to move ahead on a project, as does taking a sidestep and working on a different one. To that end, I'll be in Ukraine for a bit with a journalist friend who works for the BBC. We're doing a big piece on the Russia-Ukraine situation.

I'll be in touch. I hope you're well, Ruby.

Dexter

It hadn't made her blush from happiness, but from embarrassment, because Dexter clearly wanted to take a step back from working so closely with her. She read it in his tone, and she felt it in her gut. It was true that she'd left New York kind of abruptly and without explanation, but in the moment it had seemed like the right thing to do, to get some perspective, as Dexter is doing now.

The women laugh at something Heather has just said and Ruby smiles, hoping that she looks less like she's lost in her own thoughts than she is. There's no reason for her to feel stressed about Dexter taking a step back to work on a side project, except for the obvious potential danger of him being in an area filled with civil and political unrest. Selfishly, there's also the idea that she's entrusted him with her deepest, darkest secrets and her true emotions about some of the most challenging and important parts of her life, and he's just roaming the earth with them all in his back pocket. An image fills her brain of Dexter having a drink with a group of other journalists in a war-torn country, sitting around a table in a dark bar and knocking back shots as they share stories. She doesn't think he would divulge any of her secrets under normal circumstances, but perhaps as the alcohol loosens his tongue, he might inadvertently offer some details about her and her life. And wouldn't that be a juicy piece of gossip to trade while gunfire blasts outside the bar, the threat of danger more imminent with every passing moment? The former First Lady's secrets would be at least mildly entertaining to the journalists gathered there, exhausted and homesick as they try to amuse one another.

"What do you think, Ruby?" Molly asks, pulling her back to the present moment.

"Sorry?" Ruby pats the corner of her mouth with a napkin. "I got lost in thought there for a second."

"We were talking about the book," Sunday says. "What did you think about the protagonist needing to tell her mother-in-law off before the older woman died? We all thought it sounded cathartic as hell." The entire group laughs, remembering their own mothers-in-law. "I'd give my right arm to bring Peter's mother back to life long enough to give her a piece of my mind."

Ruby gives a half-smile. She could think of a few bones she might have to pick with Jack's late mother, but none of that really interests her at the moment. "What would you all think of taking our drinks down to the beach and listening to the ocean?" Ruby asks. "Sometimes all I can think about is that Jack died alone in the water. When I hear the waves, I wonder if they were the last thing he heard."

The other women make alarmed eye contact, clearly curious about Ruby's slightly out of character behavior.

"Sure, Rubes, we could go for a stroll," Sunday says gently, nodding encouragingly at the other women. "If what you need is to be up and moving, then we can do that. We could walk off some of this fried rice and booze. Let's do it." She stands up and walks over to the table. "I'll top off drinks if anyone wants them," Sunday says, starting with her own cup.

"I just want to be outside, walking under the moon." Ruby looks at her lap. "I need to know what Jack wanted me to do. I don't know how to figure out what he wanted, because he never told me. That letter should have been pages and pages longer, but it wasn't, so now I'm just left here to spin my wheels and guess." She spreads her hands like she has no idea what to think.

"Come on," Sunday says, walking over and offering Ruby her hand. "Up you go."

The women cross Seadog Lane by the light of the moon and stars, holding their cups as they cross the sand and head for the water.

Once they get to the shoreline, Ruby stands alone, facing the waves and not speaking for a long time. Heather and Marigold kick off their shoes and wade out to their shins as they hold hands. Molly sits on a log with Vanessa and Tilly, who have gone quiet, eyes wide as they watch the former First Lady staring at the sea. They've each gone through their own heartaches, their own sorrows. Every woman on that beach knows what it's like to fall headfirst into a deep well of feelings without warning.

"Hey, we're right here," Sunday says softly at Ruby's side as she puts an arm around her waist and rests her head on her friend's shoulder. "Whatever you have going on, we're right here, okay?"

Ruby nods, unblinking as she looks at the water and thinks about Jack. She's kept herself so busy with moving, with the bookstore, with her girls, and with Dexter and the book...so busy that the dark thoughts have barely had a chance to creep in. And yet here she is, unexpectedly tangled in the web of heartache that surrounds the unexpected death of a man she thought she knew.

Unbidden, tears start to fall. Sunday takes Ruby's hand and lets her cry.

The other women stay right where they are, their quiet support wrapping around Ruby as she lets her feelings wash over her.

I'll be okay, I'll be okay, I'll be okay, she thinks. *I've got this island and I've got these women and my girls are safe and everything will be fine...no matter what.*

Ruby knows this is true, because it has to be true. She puts her arm around Sunday and pulls her closer for comfort, glancing around at each of the other women as they bask in the moonlight.

Each and every one of us is going through our own life story, and we will all *be okay.*

Dexter

Ukraine is just as Dexter expected: fraught with tension. It's been raining and forty-seven degrees for what feels like a month of Sundays, and he sits in the lobby of the hotel in the Green Zone, surrounded by other reporters drinking coffee from small, mismatched cups and saucers. While wholly sufficient, the hotel is not plush by anyone's standards. The linens are clean and the restaurant serves hearty food that fills Dexter up at every meal, but the heavy potatoes, breads, and stews have caused him to put on a few pounds already. He's grown fond of Chicken Kyiv and beer, and each night he sits at the same table by the window in the lobby, his dinner on the plate in front of him as he types on his laptop and listens to John Coltrane on his AirPods.

It's the week after Thanksgiving, which he and Theo marked by drinking together at the bar (though of course Thanksgiving means nothing to Theo, as a Brit, he'd still been happy to drink and toast to the holiday with his old friend). Now Dexter has his mind on Christmas in the city, and he's missing the decorations in New York, and the skaters in Rockefeller Center, clad in scarves and hats and mittens. He'd even kill for a little Christmas music, but all they play at this hotel is some kind of folk music with what sounds like a lute, and it's already grating on his nerves.

A woman from the newspaper *Le Figaro* in France walks by his table, nodding at him. On Dexter's first night at the hotel she'd sent him over a drink, an overture that he knew amongst lonely, far from home journalists to mean "let's spend the night together." He'd lifted the drink in her direction and then gone right back to his laptop. Since then, she's nodded at him and smiled, clearly hoping that he might still change his mind and spend an evening or two with her.

But he won't. Dexter knows himself, and he knows why he's in Ukraine. He and Theo have been hard at work on a story about the civilians fighting to save their country from a Russian invasion, and Theo, as the lead reporter on the story, is the one to go out for days at a time, leaving Dexter behind to capture the local story and to file the updates they have so far to the BBC.

This morning, instead of walking by as she's done every time since he'd rebuffed her, the journalist from *Le Figaro* pauses at Dexter's table and looks down at him intently.

"Good morning," she says, sounding almost shy. "Maxine Ledieux, *Le Figaro*."

"Dexter North," he says, offering a hand for her to shake as he stands up from his chair, holding his napkin in the other hand. He feels a bit put out by her persistence, but his manners prevent him from rebuffing her entirely for a second time. "Pleasure to meet you."

"May I?" Maxine nods at the empty chair across from his. The table is small, round, more the height of a coffee table than a dining table, and flanked by two well-worn crushed velvet wingback chairs in burgundy.

Dexter nods his assent and she sits, crossing her legs and motioning for the server to drop off another small pot of coffee, which materializes almost immediately.

"I've been wondering what angle you're working on here," Maxine says. "I know your work in general, and of course I read your book about Monica Lewinsky, like every other curious human on the planet."

Dexter bows his head slightly in gratitude. "I'm pleased so many people found it worth reading."

"It was a stunning piece," Maxine says with a thick French accent, lifting her teacup daintily and eyeing him over the rim. "It would have been so easy to take the subject and turn her into a clown, or a foil for a fallen president. But you didn't. Instead, you treated her like a real person with real human feelings."

Dexter chuckles. "Well, she is. And in getting to know her, I found her even more human than most. She never once tried to make excuses for her actions, nor did she blame Clinton or anyone else. I enjoyed writing that book more than I can tell you."

"I felt your joy while reading it. It came across as insightful rather than exploitative, is what I'm trying to say. Someone with less experience and class would have butchered it. So kudos to you." Maxine lifts her coffee cup much the way Dexter had lifted the drink she'd sent to his table.

In her mirthful eyes, he can see that she's silently referring to that evening with this gesture, and perhaps hoping that this coffee might lead to a kind of collaboration, if you will. But it won't, and Dexter already knows that. Maxine is beautiful, and at another point in his life, it might have gone somewhere. With her long, graceful limbs, slim neck encircled with shining gold chains, and the very Parisian way she wears her clothes —the fabric complimenting her figure as if her clothing were cut specifically for her body—Dexter can feel himself eyeing her with interest, but his mind has been on Ruby for months now. And while he's refused to entertain any thoughts of Ruby that even hint at being sexual, he can't deny that he's interested in her as more than a subject for a book, which means that he has no real interest in Maxine. It's simply how he is, and how he's always been.

"I appreciate the flattery," Dexter says, pouring more hot coffee from the small pot into his cup.

"What are you working on now--other than covering Ukraine and Russia?" Maxine sits back in her chair comfortably, holding her saucer in one hand and the teacup in the other. She strikes Dexter as a French woman who spent time in her youth at an English boarding school.

It's not top secret news, given that his publisher has already sent him the advance for his book, so he tells her the truth: "I'm writing a book about Jack Hudson, but the entire piece is recreated through the lens of the First Lady. I'm looking at the way her youth and her life before marrying Jack informed her and shaped her into the kind of woman who becomes First Lady, and then I'm taking her firsthand account of how she felt after the President's suicide and using it to tell the story of Jack Hudson's fall from grace."

Maxine shakes her head and clucks to herself. "Such a tragic figure," she says, her pretty dark brows knitted together. She's no older than Dexter, and perhaps even a few years younger, but there's something blank about her face that leaves him cold; despite traveling the world and seeing war with her own eyes, Maxine is still young--she has no personal mileage.

"Tragic? Who--Jack Hudson?" Dexter asks, lifting his coffee cup.

"No, his widow," Maxine says with a slight shake of her head. "Moving to an island to hide out from the world, opening a bookshop." She wrinkles her nose like she's smelled something rotten. "Women without an education are left with nothing when the powerful men they've tied themselves to are gone."

Dexter can feel something rising inside of him and he knows that it won't end well if he opens his mouth and lets it out. Instead, he nods slowly and takes another long sip of his coffee, thinking. When he finally sets the mug on the table, he speaks. "As it turns out, Ruby Hudson attended UCLA and got an English degree." Maxine lifts one eyebrow skeptically. "She's extremely well-read and thoughtful. I think you'll find, if and when you read the book, that she's nothing like what you think she is. Moving to Shipwreck Key and starting over--opening the bookshop, letting her daughters move down there with her in their time of need--was a brave move on her part. Not every woman can recover from something as shocking as her husband's blatant infidelity and his suicide in front of the entire world, and then start her own second act without missing a beat. Ruby is a remarkable woman."

Maxine sets her cup and saucer on the table and leans forward, resting her elbow on her knee as she looks Dexter in the eye. "Sounds like she has a true fan in you, Dexter North. Better watch out so that your admiration doesn't taint your reporting." Maxine stands and smooths her loose linen pants with both hands as she gives Dexter a tiny smile. "It was lovely chatting with you."

Dexter watches as she walks back through the small lobby and climbs the stairs, her long fingers holding the chipped banister as she ascends and disappears from view.

"Was it something I said?" he mutters to himself, looking around to see if anyone else has noticed the lovely Maxine's hasty retreat. Not that he cares, but he's sure it looks like he said something to offend her, when in truth all he'd done was defend another woman.

Dexter looks out the rain-streaked window at the street outside the hotel. There are cars moving hesitantly down the street the same way the pedestrians do; everyone and everything that he's seen so far on this journey appears to be hunched over and trying to hide in plain sight. He's certainly getting the different perspective that he'd hoped for when Theo first pitched this trip to him, but now that he's here, he's had enough. He needs to finish this reporting and get back to his real life. He wants to get back to New York, maybe even take a quick jaunt to Christmas Key to lay in the sun and warm his cold bones after spending time in this cold, gray place, and most of all, he wants to get back to working with Ruby.

Sunday

Sunday is floating on her back in the Gulf of Mexico, looking up at the December sky. She's been on Shipwreck Key now for six full months, and it feels more like home to her than Washington ever did. In fact, D.C. is at least a million miles away right now for Sunday, with her ears submerged in the water and only the sounds of ocean life to accompany her thoughts.

So much has happened in these months, and Sunday feels like a different person than she was the Easter she spent searching the White House for Peter, finding him in *flagrante delicto* with another man. She's also a different person from the one who felt as if she'd lost a daughter and was barely hanging on to the other one. Now, she and her girls are in touch all the time, and over the months since their trip to Tangier Island, both Cameron and Olive have reached out to her with further questions about Benjamin and with thoughts about whether or not Ruby should ever try to find him. She personally feels the way she always has: that if he wants to find her then he will. But she loves hearing her daughters' opinions and thoughts, and she is more than willing to answer any questions they might have about her life. It's the least she can do.

A wave lifts her weightless body and sends her drifting sideways on the current, but she doesn't fight it. The sky overhead is so blue that it looks like it goes on infinitely into the heavens, with not a cloud in sight. It's the perfect morning, and while the water is cool, it's also refreshing and crisp. This is the way Sunday wants to start all her days until the end of time, and she comes out here as often as she can and floats just like this. Some days Banks jogs by and she swims to shore to talk to him briefly, and other days she doesn't even bother to lift her head out of the water until she's ready to swim in and wrap herself in a towel.

But now it's three weeks before Christmas, and both Cameron and Olive have come down to the island to spend a long weekend with her. She'd told them that there was no guarantee they'd get any holiday shopping done, unless they were looking for Jolly Roger themed gifts to give the people on their lists, but they'd both said they didn't mind, and that they wanted to come down and get away from their real lives for a few days anyway.

Sunday climbs out of the water and walks over to where she left her towel on the sun-warmed sand, shaking it out before she squeezes her hair with it and then wraps it around her body.

The beach is totally empty as she crosses the sand and climbs the steps to her house. The door to the kitchen is flung wide open, and when she walks in, she sees that one of the girls has already plugged in the Christmas tree lights. Their voices drift to her from down the hallway, where the sound of water running in the bathroom competes with the television, which is on in the front room.

Sunday stands there in her wet bathing suit and towel, appreciating the happy noise of the television, the shower, and her daughters' voices. This is a moment she could have only hoped for just months ago, and now she has it right here, in the palm of her hand. It's almost too good to be true.

"Mom? Is that you?" Cameron comes down the hall with one hand on her growing belly. She rubs it constantly and without even realizing that she's doing it. "Hey, I made crepes while you were in the water, and there's hot coffee in the pot."

Sunday smiles at her older daughter, grateful for her presence in a way that is so physical that she feels it throughout her entire body. Cameron's beautiful dark hair is pulled up into a loose topknot, and her

Guatemalan heritage means that her skin takes on the most gorgeous caramel shade after just a few days in the sun.

"Thanks, babe," Sunday says, tightening her towel around her body. She pads back into the kitchen and pours herself a mug of hot coffee. With a smile, she notes that Olive and Cameron have dug through her boxes and unearthed her holiday tea towels, leaving a red one with a Santa in a sled hanging over the edge of the sink, and a green one embroidered with a rainbow of Christmas lights is looped through the handle of the oven. There's an apple cinnamon candle burning in the center of her round kitchen table, and each place is set with a red and green plaid placemat and matching napkin.

"Mom," Cameron calls out from the front room. "Dad is on TV! You gotta see this."

Sunday finishes pouring cream into her coffee and stirs it with a spoon. She puts the cream back into the fridge and drops the spoon in the sink with a clang. She's in no hurry; she's seen Peter on television more times than she can count.

"Coming," Sunday says softly, sipping from her overly full mug as she walks into the front room.

Cameron is sitting on the couch with one bare foot pulled up under her, and one hand resting on her belly. Next to her on the end table is a cup of tea. "Come, sit," she says to Sunday, patting the couch beside her. Sunday sits.

"And you're officially announcing your bid for the Oval Office this morning?" the newscaster—a beautiful redhead with perfect makeup and just the right combination of inquisitiveness and seriousness—asks Peter as he sits in a chair across from her with his legs crossed at the knee.

"I am," Peter Bond says, giving her one firm nod. "I think the four years I spent as Vice President give me the background and the understanding of what it means to be President, and that's a definite advantage for the American public." He turns and looks directly into the camera. "When you vote for Peter Bond, you're casting a vote of confidence and support for the good work that Jack Hudson and I did as a team during his term in the Oval Office. I was Jack's right-hand man, and everything I learned and everything I'll bring to the job are things that I learned from him."

Sunday feels her damp bathing suit against her skin under the towel, but she's not cold. She holds her mug with both hands, not drinking the coffee, but instead watching the man she'd been married to for over thirty years as he does his best to show the viewing public the man that they could have as President, if they feel so inclined to cast their vote in his favor.

"Do you think Dad could actually pull this off?" Cameron asks as the redhead lobs another question at Peter.

Sunday turns her head to look at her lovely daughter. "I think he really could," she admits. "Your father is a politician to his very core, and I mean that in a flattering way." Peter hadn't always taken his role as Vice President seriously and Sunday knows that, but there were times that she watched him and knew that his position was simply one of back-up anyway. He was part of the establishment, but at times he was just the Prince Harry to the Prince William, and his impishness and relaxed attitude reminded her of how extraneous he was.

Cameron laughs. "Yeah, I guess being considered a true politician could go either way, couldn't it?"

"Absolutely." Sunday sips her hot coffee.

The tree is twinkling just to the left side of the television, which is mounted above the small fireplace, and for a second she looks at the tree, losing herself in the flicker of the white fairy lights. The frost and glitter of all the handmade ornaments catches her eye, courtesy of all the years that her daughters brought them home from school, as well as the shiny rhinestone star that she places atop the tree each year.

Memories of past Christmases come flooding back to her as Peter levels his gaze at the interviewer on the screen, speaking earnestly about his stance on gun control. Sunday watches his lips move for a just a moment before the image of him morphs into one in her mind of him sitting next to their Christmas tree in the small house they'd purchased in D.C. just after adopting both girls. Peter, clad only in plaid pajama bottoms and a Penn State sweatshirt, is putting together a Barbie house on the floor next to the twinkling tree, and Olive and Cameron are sitting together in matching holiday-themed pajamas, squealing with glee over their new stuffed animals and dolls.

"Daddy?" Cameron says in Sunday's reverie, "Do you think Barbie is pretty?" The tiny girl holds up a blonde, curvy doll for her father's inspection. Peter's eyes flick up from the dollhouse construction and land on the Barbie. "Not as pretty as you," he says, winking at her. Cameron smiles with pride.

As Sunday remembers this scene now, she also remembers the barest, most fleeting thought that had skipped through her mind like a stone skimming over a pond: *Of course he doesn't think Barbie is pretty,* she'd thought in that moment, *but he wouldn't mind a date with Ken.* She blinks now as the whole scene comes flooding back to her. In her mind and in her heart, Sunday had known for years that Peter preferred men—how could she not have known?—a woman's instincts are almost always stronger than she gives herself credit for. She'd known, and she'd pushed it aside. And looking back now, she's not even sorry. She's been fortunate enough to raise two girls and to give them a life they never would have known otherwise, not to mention the fact that she's gotten to live an incredible life, one that almost no one else gets to experience. So she's not sorry, not one bit, that she chose to look past the obvious truth and to stay with Peter as long as she did.

"But we understand that you're going through a divorce now, and that Mrs. Bond is currently living in Florida and will not be joining you on the campaign trail." The redhead is looking at Peter with a gaze so intense that Sunday is ripped back to the present, all memories of a younger Peter piecing together a dollhouse forced out of her mind's eye. She watches the screen, listening and waiting for his response.

"All true," Peter confirms with one crisp nod. "Sunday and I are separated amicably, and while she will not be scheduled to join me for any of my official events, she's always invited to attend, and she knows that."

Next to Sunday, Cameron huffs in disbelief. "Come on," she says under her breath.

"He has to say that, babe." Sunday reaches over and pats her daughter's bare thigh, but she doesn't tear her eyes away from the screen. Certainly Peter can say whatever he wants, as she wasn't able to extract a promise from him that he wouldn't disclose anything about her life or her past.

She holds her breath, waiting to see which way this interview will go.

"What do you think the former Second Lady has up her sleeve now? Does she have future plans—maybe to help the former First Lady run her bookshop?" The interviewer smiles for the first time, and Sunday can see her relax a little.

Peter holds his answer for a beat, and Sunday knows him well enough to know that he's deciding right then and there what he'll say about her. Her heart picks up its pace in anticipation.

"Sunday is a talented woman who lives for her family," Peter says carefully. "We're expecting our first grandchild in the new year, so I would imagine that she's looking forward to that. Believe it or not, she still offers me bits and pieces of advice, and I take them under advisement." His eyes lock in on the camera again, but just briefly, and Sunday knows exactly what he's referring to: the moment in the lawyer's office in Miami where she advised him to come out and tell the world who he really is. He won't do it, and she knows that now as she watches his face, but he'd heard her, and he knows that the people closest to him are aware of who he truly is, for better or worse, and that's all that matters.

"Congratulations," the interviewer says, beaming at Peter. "That's wonderful news about your first grandchild."

"Thank you. And Sunday has a long history with adoption," Peter goes on, glancing at her through the camera again. "I'd love to see her work with our friends at the National Council for Adoption to see if she can put her experience to use promoting all the wonderful ways that adoption helps build families. It certainly helped to build ours."

The interviewer smiles her thousand-watt smile at Peter and thanks him for his time, closing out by turning to the camera and saying a few things about her upcoming shows and guests, but Sunday is sitting there stunned.

"Mom," Olive says. She's come into the room and has been standing next to the couch, watching the interview alongside Sunday and Cameron. "That's an awesome idea—you totally should."

"He meant *all* of your experience with adoption, didn't he?" Cameron asks, turning her body on the couch so that she's facing Sunday. "Benjamin, too, right?"

Sunday nods, looking at both of her girls. "I think so." She's still gobsmacked by Peter's words, and the idea that she could do something as important as work with the National Council for Adoption. Utilizing her former platform as Second Lady isn't something she's taken seriously up until this point because she's been so busy worrying about how to climb out of the deep ditch of her marriage. But with this suggestion from Peter, she's actually considering it. "I mean...I could do that, couldn't I?" she asks hesitantly. "I could even tell my story—my whole story—and help people."

Olive plops down on the couch right between her mother and sister. "Yes!" she says enthusiastically. "You can do anything, Mom. We believe in you."

"Go for it, Mom. You've got this," Cameron says, leaning forward so she can look at Sunday from the other end of the couch. "I think you should definitely do it."

Rather than just a prickling of tears, Sunday feels the full onslaught of joy gushing from her eyes and she laughs. "Thank you, girls. Thank you for finding me, and for letting me be your mom."

The three women wrap their arms around each other in a tear-filled group hug right there on the couch, with the white lights twinkling and with Sunday's damp towel and bathing suit reminding her that she still needs to change and eat breakfast.

"Knock knock," comes a man's voice from the kitchen. Sunday disentangles from her girls and jumps up, tightening the towel around her body just as Banks peeks into the front room. "Sorry," he says, looking guilty as he hooks a thumb over his shoulder, "your back door was open, and I was running by."

"No, come in, come in," Sunday says, holding her towel around herself modestly, as she wonders whether her hair is plastered to her head and if her makeup-free morning face is too scary for Banks to see.

"Actually," he says with an impish grin. "I was thinking of taking a plunge in the water, and I wanted to see if you felt like a swim. There's no rip current today," he adds with a wink.

Sunday looks down at her towel. "I'm already dressed for it," she says, feeling a surge of carefree joy fill her body. For the first time since she came in from the beach, goosebumps cover her arms, but she's still not cold. "Might as well head out for another dip."

Olive stands up. "We'll make more crepes," she says with a smile. "Banks, you want some?"

"Love some. Thank you," he says, his eyes still on Sunday. "Shall we?"

With one quick look back at the television screen where Peter is sitting there with his calm, practiced politician's smile, she follows Banks through the sun-warmed kitchen and out onto the sand.

The rest of her life awaits her, and suddenly it's filled with exciting question marks and wonderful unknowns, like what good works she'll do, and what her life will be like as a grandmother. The thought of holding a new baby in her arms, sweet-smelling and the very embodiment of hope and true love, makes her want to shout to the world how wonderful it is to be alive, to be human, to be a woman.

But for the time being, the most exciting thing that awaits her is the cool, exhilarating sensation of the December waves on her skin, and the promise of hot crepes at her kitchen table with her beloved daughters and a gorgeous man. They'll laugh and talk and drink coffee together as the sun spills through her kitchen windows and the Christmas tree lights dance and glimmer with cheer in the very next room.

For the first time in as long as she can remember, Sunday doesn't feel the need to run away from anything.

She's finally home.

Come back to Shipwreck Key...

Marigold Pim, former supermodel, refuses to let society dictate her worth. She is embracing life and using her public platform to advocate for a very unpopular path: aging gracefully. She's also looking for love in Book Three—available on Amazon and in Kindle Unlimited!

Also by Stephanie Taylor

Stephanie also writes a long-running romantic comedy series set on a fictional key off the coast of Florida. Christmas Key is a magical place that's decorated for the holidays all year round, and you'll instantly fall in love with the island and its locals.

To see a complete list of the Christmas Key series along with all of Stephanie's other books, please visit:

Stephanie Taylor's Books

To hear about any new releases, sign up here and you'll be the first to know!

About the Author

Stephanie Taylor is a high-school teacher who loves sushi, "The Golden Girls," Depeche Mode, orchids, and coffee. She is the author of the Christmas Key books, a romantic comedy series about a fictional island off the coast of Florida, as well as The Holiday Adventure Club series, and the Shipwreck Key series.

https://redbirdsandrabbits.com
redbirdsandrabbits@gmail.com

Made in the USA
Coppell, TX
20 January 2025

44686776R00105